They hurtled out of the bedroom door and across the living-room, hand-in-hand, but they were far too slow, and it was far too late. A huge dark shape came lunging towards them, and Kelly felt Kevin whipped away from her. "*Kelly*!" he screamed, but Kelly herself fell sideways, off-balance, and hit her back against the arm of the sofa.

"*Kelly! It's got me! Kelly*!"

She could hear Kevin's feet drumming against the wall, and she could vaguely see the shape that was holding him down. It was black and hairy and indistinct, and it smelled so foul that the bile rose up in the back of her throat.

She was terrified. Her every instinct was to run. But Kevin was kicking and screaming and she knew that she couldn't leave him.

"*Kelly! It's crushing me, Kelly! Kelly, do something for God's sake*!"

Point Horror has mutated...

Ortho's Brood
Roger Davenport

Night of the Toxic Slime
Antony Masters

Dissolvers
Crawlers
Andrew Matthews

Carnival of the Dead
Laurence Staig

MUTANT *Point Horror*

Hair Raiser

Graham Masterton

SCHOLASTIC

Scholastic Children's Books,
Commonwealth House, 1–19 New Oxford Street,
London WC1A 1NU, UK
a division of Scholastic Ltd
London ~ New York ~ Toronto ~ Sydney ~ Auckland
Mexico City ~ New Delhi ~ Hong Kong

First published in the UK by Scholastic Ltd, 2001

ISBN 0 439 99919 7

Typeset by TW Typesetting, Midsomer Norton, Somerset
Printed by Cox & Wyman Ltd, Reading, Berks.

10 9 8 7 6 5 4 3 2 1

1

"I saw a rat!" screamed Kelly. "I'm sure I saw a rat!"

"Where? Where? I can't stand rats!" said Susan. She was halfway back up the stairs already.

Kelly peered into the gloom at the opposite end of the basement. This was where all the black plastic bags of rubbish were stored, before they took them out for the dustmen. All of the crumpled silver foils which had been used for highlighting their customers' hair, all the empty bottles of shampoo and conditioner, all the paper towels and cotton wool. And – of course – all of the hair which Kelly had to sweep up from the salon floor – blonde, black, ginger, mousy and grey.

"I'll go and tell Simon," said Susan, opening the door that led to the brightly-lit salon.

"No, don't! Not while we've got customers here! He'll go crazy!"

Kelly picked up the broom which was leaning against the basement wall and poked at the nearest bag of rubbish. She listened, but she heard nothing except the crinkling of foil. She prodded the bag next to it, which was fatter and softer and crammed with hair. Nothing stirred.

"You're imagining it," said Susan. "You won't find any rats in here. You know what Simon's like. He's absolutely fanatical about keeping the place clean."

Kelly took two more cautious steps forward. There was a brick arch in the far corner of the basement, and beyond the arch it was so dark that anything could have been hiding in there and she wouldn't have been able to see what it was.

She prodded the broom handle into the blackness as far as she dared – irrationally afraid that something would snatch it out of her grasp. Then she backed away, her heart beating so fast that it felt as if it were going to trip over itself. She knew that a rat would probably be just as frightened as she was, but that didn't make her feel any braver. Her brother Kieran was always telling her that she was thousands of times bigger than the biggest spider, but that didn't stop her from screaming when she found a big black hairy one crouching in the bath.

"Come on," Susan urged her. "Simon's next lady

will be here in a minute, and you know how he likes to have his station all tidied up."

Kelly retreated towards the staircase, keeping her broom lifted just in case. She had already climbed up three stairs when she heard the noise again. It wasn't so much of a scampering sound – more of a soft, furtive stirring.

"Did you hear that?" she whispered.

"What? I didn't hear anything."

"I'm sure there's something down here. Supposing it's one of Mrs Marshall's kittens from upstairs? It might have got itself stuck in one of the bags."

She went back to the heap of rubbish and listened again. "Come *on*," Susan insisted. "I've just heard Simon calling you!"

"But suppose it's a kitten and it's trapped and it's suffocating? I can't just leave it here, can I?"

She prodded the distended bag of hair. She was sure that she could hear movement inside it. She hesitated a moment and then she laid her hand on it. She had always been a bold girl. Through the plastic she could feel all of the crunchy clumps and swept-up curls. She pressed the bag harder and then she patted it, hard, two or three times – and then she definitely felt it stir.

"It's here, Susan! It's in here!"

She broke a small hole in the plastic with her fingernail. *Please don't let it be a huge great rat*, she prayed. *Not one of those greasy brown sewer rats with horrible rings around their tails and red eyes and yellow teeth.*

She tore the hole a little wider. A few clumps of chopped-off hair dropped out over her shoes and up her sleeve. She poked the bag with the end of her broom, although the hair was very spongy and difficult to penetrate.

Suddenly she felt an enormous *heave*, like somebody turning over in bed – and she called out, "Susan!" – jumping and stumbling away from the bag, her whole body quivering with fright.

At that moment the door at the top of the stairs was thrown wide open and Simon Crane called out, "Kelly! Get a move on! Mrs Baxter's here and my station looks like a bomb's hit it!"

He came downstairs and looked around the basement. "What's this?" he wanted to know, kicking at the hair that had spilled out of the bag. "One of your jobs is to keep this place tidy, not make it worse than it is already!"

"I'm sorry, Mr Crane. I'll sweep it all up."

"Well, leave it till later. And, please, Miss O'Sullivan, do start calling me 'Simon', for goodness' sake."

"Yes, Mr Crane. I mean Simon."

Simon Crane was tall and very thin with long blond hair brushed loosely into curls. He had a sharp, handsome face with blue eyes and a long straight nose. He always wore tight black trousers and a black shirt with the collar turned up at the back, and a large silver chain around his neck. Kelly hadn't been able to believe her luck when he offered her a job as a trainee. Not only was he gorgeous, but he used to work in Richard Walker's salon in the West End of London, and he was a brilliant hair stylist. She often wondered why he had come out here to open a salon in the suburbs, but whatever the reason, she was glad that he had.

"I was wondering if I could go half an hour early tonight," she asked him, as they climbed the stairs back up to the salon. "It's my brother's birthday party and I haven't bought him a present yet."

"All right, then … as long as everything's cleaned up. When you've sorted my station out you can clean the backwash basins and make sure there's plenty of paper in the toilets."

Kelly hesitated, and then she said, "Downstairs … I think there might be a rat."

"A *rat*? What are you talking about?"

"I heard a noise when I was putting the rubbish away. A sort of rustling."

"Well, I don't know what it was. But we've never had rats."

"I'm sure I heard *something*."

Simon said, "Don't worry. It was probably a bird stuck in the chimney. That happens, now and again. Now, come on, chop-chop, let's get moving. We've got a really crazy day today."

Kelly turned back to close the basement door. As she did so, she thought she saw a shadow flickering across the wall, only to be swallowed up in the darkness beyond the arch. She looked across at Simon, but he was already smiling and chatting to Mrs Baxter. She thought of interrupting him, but she didn't want to make a fool of herself, and so she said nothing, although she closed the door firmly and made sure that she locked it.

She went to his station and rearranged all of his scissors and bottles of styling products. She knew that she would have to go back down into the basement later today, to finish sweeping up, and she wasn't looking forward to it at all.

After the last customer had left, Simon locked the front door and switched off the purple neon sign outside. It read *Sissuz Unisex Hair Stylists* and featured a large pair of scissors with snipping blades. Susan and Kevin put away all of their combs and brushes, while Kelly gave the floor one last sweep.

"And don't forget downstairs, will you?" Simon reminded her – as if she could forget.

Kelly had always wanted to be a vet rather than a hairdresser. She adored animals, particularly dogs and horses, and whenever they visited her uncle's farm in County Kerry she spent most of her time in the stables. But the O'Sullivans were a large family – five brothers and two sisters – and her parents hadn't been able to afford to send her to veterinary college.

"We have to choose between education in our heads or shoes on our feet," her father had told her. "And I'm afraid that the shoes win, hands down." Her father was always saying things like that.

So now Kelly was trying to save up her tuition fees, and enough money to find herself a flat. That was one of the reasons she liked working for Simon. He always showed an interest in her, and whenever he had a few minutes to spare, he would show her the basics of good hair styling. He had already taught her to feather her own fringe, and how to cut in layers. When she graduated to stylist herself, she would be earning three times as much money, with tips.

"Come on, let's get on with it," said Simon, counting the last of the day's takings out of the till. "You don't want to be here all night, do you?"

He checked his gold Rolex watch. "Listen, I have to rush. I'm ten minutes late for my photo shoot already. I'm doing all the hair for the *Wedding Bells* catalogue. Make sure you switch the alarm on before you leave."

"Yes, Simon," said Susan – and, after he had walked out of the door, "Three bags full of hair, Simon."

"Don't you like him?" asked Kelly.

"Oh, he's all right," said Susan. "He's bossy, that's all. And he really thinks that he's God's gift to hairdressing."

"He's been really nice to me."

They heard Simon close the back door of the salon and they heard him starting up his BMW. Susan said, "Is that the time? Listen Kelly, I've got to shoot off, too. I would have stayed and given you a hand, but I promised to babysit for Desmond and Marie. You know how to put the alarm on, don't you?"

Susan was Jamaican. She was tall and slim and very pretty, with hair that was always fantastically decorated with beads and ribbons and combs. She was equally skilled with white and black hair, and one day she wanted to open her own multi-racial hair salon, Chessboard. She was always joking and fooling around, and hardly a day went by when she didn't make Kelly breathless with laughter.

Kevin said, "I've got to go, too, I'm afraid. Michael and me are going to the cinema. He's dying to see this Japanese arthouse movie. Something about samurai warriors, with subtitles. Personally, I'd rather go and see *Titanic* again. At least you're guaranteed a good cry."

Kevin was pale-faced, a little overweight, with a shock of curly blond hair which he had highlighted himself. He lived alone in a flat over The Light of India restaurant, and went on walking holidays, and he was probably the kindest, least affected person that Kelly had ever met. More than once he had shared his lunch with her, even though he was on a diet and it was only lettuce sandwiches on wholemeal bread. After lunch he went out to the local newsagent and bought eight Snickers bars – two for her and six for him. "The thing about diets is that you've got to creep up on them," he said.

Kevin and Susan waved Kelly goodnight and noisily left. She heard them laughing as they walked across the car park. Now she was alone in the salon, with only the fitful buzzing of a faulty fluorescent light for company. She walked along to the front desk, straightening the four revolving chairs and making sure that every station had its display shelves fully stocked with shampoo, conditioner, hair gel and all the other products they sold. They made a lot of profit out of them, and Simon was always talking about bringing out his own range. "I mean, what's in them? Only water and lauryl sulphate, and you can sell them for fourteen quid a bottle."

On the wall of the salon was a huge blown-up black-and-white photograph of Elizabeth Green, the actress, hair by Simon Crane. He had given her his "flower-fairy" cut, which made her hair look like petals. But these days nobody like Elizabeth Green ever came to have their hair cut by Simon Crane – especially not here, at Sissuz, in this dull parade of shops in Rayner's Lane, in the grey, monotonous suburbs northwest of London.

Kelly had asked Kevin why Simon had left Richard Walker to open his own salon here, but

Kevin had shaken his head and said, "Don't ask me. And don't ask him, either. If you even *mention* the name of Richard Walker, he goes ballistic."

Kelly put off going down to the basement for as long as she could. But it was well past six o'clock now, and it was already dark outside, and she still had to go and buy that U2 CD for little Patrick.

She peered at herself in one of the mirrors. She didn't *look* frightened. She was a petite girl – 5ft 2½ins in her popsocks but she always said she was 5ft 3ins and when she wore her really high heels from Shelley's she claimed that she was 5ft 5ins. She had masses of thick golden-red hair, like all of the O'Sullivan girls. It was soft and gleaming and when she brushed it out her father said that it looked as if the summer sun were setting behind her head.

She had never thought that she was pretty. When she was thirteen, she had seriously believed that she would never have a boyfriend, ever. In fact she thought she was almost a freak. Her nose was too snubby. She had too many freckles. Her legs were as skinny as one of her uncle's newborn foals, and as for her figure, she was still going to school with her bra stuffed with Kleenex when the other girls looked like candidates for *Baywatch*.

But she was seventeen now and in the past four years a strange, magical thing had happened to her, almost without her noticing it. When she looked in the mirror these days she saw a young woman with eyes as green as glass and a perfect nose and one of those pink, bow-shaped mouths that looked as if she had just been kissed. And as for her figure – well, these days she needed to use Kleenex only to wipe off her eye make-up or blow her nose.

She felt much more confident these days, too, although she still hadn't found herself a boyfriend. Most of the boys of her own age always seemed to act so stupid and young.

She looked towards the black door that led to the basement. "Come on," she told herself. "It won't take long. And what can a rat do to you, Kelly, even if it *is* a rat?" She had seen her uncle's terriers chasing rats out of the stables, and they hadn't been *that* frightening, had they? Well, yes, she had to admit to herself that they had, and she had horrible memories of the farm boys beating them to death with sticks, and all the blood and the squealing. And one of them could be waiting for her downstairs.

She opened the door and switched on the light, but there was only a single naked bulb in the basement. What it lit was still very gloomy, and what it didn't light was black and impenetrable and strange. Hunched-up shadows that could have been nothing more than hunched-up shadows – or some deformed creature from the wrong side of the night that wanted to test out its teeth on her arms and her legs. One black shape was flung up high against the opposite wall, and it looked as if it had horns and wings, but it was only the shadow of an old-fashioned helmet hair-dryer with a plastic cover flung over it.

She said a little prayer that she and her friends used to recite at school. "Dagda, protect me from evil." Dagda was the Father of All, the Lord of Knowledge and the Sun of All Sciences, the leader of the Irish fairy people.

"Oh, and God protect me, too," she added, as she took the first step down the stairs.

There was no sound in the basement except for a distant, echoing drip. Kelly stood still for a while, listening, but she heard no scratching or scuffling. Occasionally, a bus rumbled by, and then there was shouting and tinkling and laughter as some boys walked past, kicking an empty soft-drink can. But then there was silence again, except for that single *drip, drip, drip*.

Kelly approached the split-open bag, with all of its hair bulging out. Once, all of this hair had belonged to somebody. It had been part of them, part of what they looked like and who they were. They had washed it and combed it and their lovers had run their fingers through it. Now it was nothing but dead matter – rubbish, like pared-off fingernails or flakes of skin or anything else that the human body discards on its journey through life. Kelly suddenly remembered a newspaper report that she had read, about a special team of cleaners who go through the whole of the London Underground system at night, scraping human hair off the rails. Tons of it, matted and greasy. It almost has a life of its own.

She took a fresh black plastic bag from the shelf at the bottom of the stairs. She took it over to the split-open sack, dropped it on to the floor nearby and started to sweep. First of all she would collect up all of the stray cuttings. Then she would lift up the broken bag and slide it inside the new bag, tying it up tight. Then one last sweep-up, and off to the Esso garage shop to buy Patrick's CD, and home for the party.

She swept the floor thoroughly – even lifting up some of the other rubbish bags to make sure that the hair hadn't been caught underneath. She sneezed five times in quick succession.

Oh God, she thought. I've been breathing in Mrs Baxter's iron-grey hair; not to mention Mrs Patel's long black silky locks; and those tight permanent-waved curls that Mrs Philips has been asking for, ever since her husband started showing an interest in the Lady Captain of the Pinner Green Golf Club.

Her father had once told her that people think they have clearly-defined edges, but they don't. They're for ever shedding bits and pieces of them-selves, and other people will breathe in those bits and pieces. Every single time you take a breath, every single time, you're breathing in a molecule of air that was breathed in by everybody else in history, including Julius Caesar and Henry VIII and Jesus Christ. After her father had told her that, she had walked around for days with a handkerchief tied around her face, like a bank robber.

She lifted up the big bag of hair. It wasn't particularly heavy, but it was awkward. She started to push it into the new plastic bag, trying not to drop too much hair on the floor. She stopped halfway through, because she was making so much noise, so much squeaking of plastic, that she couldn't hear any other noises in the basement. She listened for a few moments, but all she heard was *drip*, *drip*, *drip*.

She had almost managed to force the bag of hair into the new bag, however, when she was sure that she heard somebody whisper.

"*Bet say lest*," followed by some words that were so muffled that she couldn't make them out. "Hello?" she said, her voice taut and bright and fearful.

There was a very long silence, and then she heard some more whispering. It was definitely French, but not like any French that Kelly had ever heard before. "Hello?" she repeated. Her voice was beginning to waver now. She couldn't think where the whispering was coming from. But then it started again – so close that it was obvious that it was coming from the bag of hair.

The voice was hoarse, urgent and dirty-sounding.

It reminded her of the middle-aged man who had tried to pick her up outside the Electric nightclub, the last time that she and her friend Jacquie had gone dancing. He had been drunk, and had staggered about, his eyes wandering around like planets.

"*What you and me could do together, darling, you don't have any idea.*" And here was the same kind of voice, coming out of this bag of hair. "*Tais-toi, folle, tais-toi.*"

The bag started to *ripple* in her hands, ripple and twist. Without any warning it burst wide open, and hair came blowing out of it in a thin, rustling stream. She covered her eyes with her hands, but she felt it covering her, soft and prickly and loathsome, and she couldn't help breathing it in, and sneezing and sneezing.

She climbed to her feet, blinded, and staggered to the right. She nearly fell, but she managed to find the wall, and then the bottom of the staircase. She opened her eyes a little and saw that the whole of the basement was thick with flying hair, a hair storm. It whirled around the naked light bulb like fine glittering rain, and settled on everything. Kelly could feel it pouring down the neck of her blouse and all over her face. She climbed up the stairs gasping because every breath she took was filled with hair. She even had hair on her tongue.

She had almost reached the top of the stairs when she swallowed a whole thistledown of hair. She stopped, coughing and gasping. She took a deep intake of breath, and all that did was to pull the hair even further into her windpipe. Panicking, desperate, she tried to cough it up, but it didn't want to be dislodged. She gagged, and made a horrible retching sound, but still the hair was stuck in her throat, and the hair still flew wildly around her.

There was a moment at the top of the stairs when she was sure that she was going to suffocate. She couldn't breathe in, she couldn't cough out. She clung on to the railing, her eyes bulging, her hand clutching her throat, and all she could think of was that little Patrick would be devastated if she choked to death, and on his birthday too.

3

Somehow, she managed to push open the salon door. She stumbled across to the backwash basins, snatched up one of the sprays, and turned it on. She sprayed herself straight in the face with her mouth wide open, so that the water gushed right down her throat. She swallowed, gagged, and swallowed again, and at last she managed to cough up a soggy lump of human hair.

She bent over the basin, spitting and spitting. She kept making awful sick-sounding noises, especially when one of the hairs stuck to the back of her throat. But after three or four minutes of drinking and spitting she began to feel better.

She looked in the mirror over the washbasin and saw that – behind her – the basement door was still slightly ajar. She didn't know what to do. Perhaps she should call the police, and tell them that there was somebody down there, hiding amongst the sacks of rubbish. But suppose she had imagined it? Supposing the whispering had been nothing more than a draught, blowing through the basement? Old Mrs Marshall who lived upstairs, she could have opened the back door, couldn't she, and that might have caused it. A draught would have blown up all of that hair, too.

She called Simon on his mobile number.

"Simon, it's Kelly."

"What's the problem? I'm right in the middle of traffic."

"Listen, can you hear me? I've just been sweeping the basement."

"Are you still at the salon? I thought you were going to go home early."

"I was. But I think there's somebody down there."

"What? What are you talking about? Who?"

"I don't know. I heard him. He was speaking French, I think."

"Kelly, there's nobody there, I can assure you. Just finish up and go home to your party, and I'll drop by the salon this evening just to make sure that everything's OK."

"I'm afraid that all the hair—"

She was about to tell him that the basement was in an even worse mess than it had been before, but he must have driven into a tunnel, because they were cut off. She waited for a moment and then she put the phone down.

She tiptoed over to the basement door, opened it a fraction more and listened. It was silent again. No voices. Only the dripping. Cautiously, she reached her hand inside and switched off the light.

At home, and end-of-terrace house in Waverley Lane, Patrick's birthday party had already started. The living-room and the kitchen were already packed with relatives and friends, far too many for a house so small, but that was what the O'Sullivans were used to, a house that was full to bursting, and that was what they enjoyed. There were balloons and streamers everywhere, and children tumbling downstairs, and their Irish setter Barney kept circling hungrily around the dining table with all of its barbecued chicken legs and spare ribs and cheesy biscuits.

Kelly's mother was in the kitchen with her Auntie Shelagh, putting the finishing touches to the birthday cake, which was supposed to be a roller boot but looked more like a hippopotamus. "Do y'know, if I purposely set out to make a cake that looked like a hippopotamus, I couldn't for the life of me," laughed Auntie Shelagh. She was big and hearty, always nudging and joking, while Kelly's mother Kathleen was delicate and small and always worried that her baking wouldn't turn out perfect.

"How was your day, darling?" Kelly's mother asked her. "You look tired. They're not making you work too hard, are they?"

"Your mother's right, it's very peaky you're looking," said Auntie Shelagh. "Are you sure you're getting enough to eat? I know what it's like with girls of your age. Living off half an orange and a strawberry yogurt."

"It's nothing," said Kelly. "It was a long day, that's all."

Kelly went past the dining-room, where her father John and all of her uncles were gathered around the sideboard drinking Guinness and cider.

"There's my princess!" declared her father, lifting his glass. "Come on in and say hello now, Kelly."

Uncle Sean was standing by the door with his bald head and his thick tweed suit and his nose like the purple bulb of an old-fashioned motor horn. "So you're a hairdresser now! I'll bet you get to hear all the gossip these days. All those middle-aged ladies, chit-chatting under the dryers."

"Not yet. I'm only a junior. I spend most of my time sweeping up."

"All that hair! I've often wondered what hairdressers do with all of that hair. Do they make mattresses out of it, perhaps? Or shoulder pads? Or wigs?"

"Uncle Sean, even you wouldn't want to wear a wig made out of the hair that *I* sweep up."

"You could pick me out the ginger bits, couldn't you? That's what I used to be, flaming red."

"Flaming stupid, more like," put in Kelly's father.

She went upstairs to the small bedroom she shared at the back of the house with her older sister Siobhan. They shared a dressing-table and all of Kelly's make-up was crowded down at one end and Siobhan's was crowded down the other, like two opposing armies. A vanilla-scented candle flickered between them. Over Siobhan's bed hung a large poster of Bono; and over Kelly's bed she had pinned an even larger poster of Leonardo di Caprio.

Kelly often longed for a room of her own but she knew that her mother and father did their best, and that they gave her all they could afford. Sometimes she wished they weren't so loving and generous: at least she would be able to feel sorry for herself.

She washed her face and brushed out her hair and changed into the little black velvet dress that she had bought from Etam for Brendan's disco party in the summer. She made it look different with long strings of pearls.

She put on her wristwatch and her charm bracelet, but as she did so she noticed that she still had five or six hairs on the back of her wrist, from the basement at Sissuz. She brushed them but they didn't come off. She brushed them again, harder this time. Then she tugged at them, between finger and thumb. They didn't come off because they seemed to have rooted themselves.

Her heart started to beat a little faster, and she began to feel breathless again, the way she had when she was choking with hair. She pulled at each individual hair, but they were all stuck fast – one of them black, one of them of grey and two mousy-coloured ones.

She sat at the dressing-table for a while, close to panic. Then she thought: come on, Kelly, this is ridiculous. Whatever she had experienced down in the basement, it must have been her own imagination. Lots of people claim to have heard voices and doors banging and things going bump in the night. Her grandmother said that she had woken up in her cottage in Sneem to see a white nun standing at the end of her bed.

Kelly believed in all kinds of supernatural things herself, like rubbing a stone on your hand to get rid of warts, and she believed in spells too, and the magic of herbs. She believed that if you looked in a mirror with a candle burning you would see your future husband standing behind you (although it hadn't worked yet – all she had seen was Siobhan's dressing-gown hanging on the back of the door).

But that voice she had heard in the basement, and all that flying hair? She just didn't know, and she wasn't at all sure that she *wanted* to know.

She opened Siobhan's drawer and took out a pair

of tweezers. She tried to tug the hairs on her wrist, but they were rooted so deeply that all she did was bring tears to her eyes. In the end, she went into the bathroom where her father's razor was standing in a tooth-glass, and shaved them off.

Back in her bedroom, she finished off her make-up. She had bought herself a new bronze lipstick called Autumn Desire and she pouted her lips and peered at herself closely in the mirror. Not bad. It suited her hair colour and it made her look much more grown-up.

She was still pouting at herself when a voice said, "Is this a face-pulling party for one, or can anybody join in?"

She looked up, startled, and there in the mirror was a tall broad-shouldered boy with black curly hair. She didn't recognize him at first, but then she turned around on her stool and said, "Ned! You're Ned! I don't believe it! The last time I saw you, you were wearing short trousers!"

"I still wear them now, when I'm playing rugby. I saw you come in. I've been waiting for you downstairs. You know – just to get acquainted again."

He came into the room and looked around. The skinny boy with the protruding ears that she remembered from seven years ago had grown into an extremely good-looking young man, with humorous brown eyes and the easiest of smiles. He even had a five o'clock shadow too, which made him look very mature.

Kelly gave her hair a last, quick brush and stood up. All of a sudden she felt desperately tongue-tied; which she never usually was, ever.

"I hear you've got a job at a hairdresser's," said Ned. "I remember you telling me that you always wanted to work with animals."

"I'm saving up for veterinary college."

"I don't know. Look at you, you're looking very glamorous tonight, don't you think? I can't imagine you sticking your hand up some cow's rear end."

"You've been watching too much James Herriot."

"Well, maybe. I'm a townie these days. I've got a job selling computers. Come downstairs and have a drink and I'll tell you all about it."

"Selling computers? That sounds boring."

"You can't say that. Boring? It's the future."

Kelly turned round to blow out the scented candle, and suddenly realized that she had seen Ned's face in a mirror, by candlelight. Perhaps he was right. Perhaps they *were* going to be talking about the future.

She was so frightened of what Simon was going to say when he saw the burst bags and the scattered hair that when she woke up the following morning she was tempted to call in sick. But the house was bustling with everybody getting ready for school or for work or whatever they were going to do. And when Kelly's mother called upstairs to say that she needed her to do some shopping at lunchtime because they were out of baked beans and fish fingers and HP sauce and sandwich bags, her conscience wouldn't allow her to lie in bed all day.

She put on a short, grey knitted dress and black tights and came downstairs with her hair tied back with a black ribbon.

"You look like you're going to a funeral," said her father, cheerfully, kissing her on the cheek.

She couldn't eat much for breakfast, only a slice of toast and thinly-spread honey. Patrick was struggling to eat three Shredded Wheat. "I'm older now. I need lots to eat."

The youngest, Martin, sat in his high-chair and made a spectacular mess with his puréed apricot, "Mum," said Kelly, "he's sticking it into his eye."

Kelly's mother was quite unperturbed. "He'll find out soon enough where his mouth is. All men do."

Kelly could walk to work in less than ten minutes, but today she dawdled. It was one of those sharp, crisp mornings in October, when the gutters are crowded with tawny leaves, and the air smells like frost and woodsmoke. Mornings like these always reminded Kelly of going back to school for the autumn term, and she supposed they always would. She missed school. She hadn't realized how daunting it was going to be, supporting herself, and making all her own decisions, even if she did still live at home.

She arrived at Sissuz five minutes late. The salon was already open and Simon was emptying bags of change into the till. He looked up at her when she came in, and made a show of checking his watch, but he didn't say anything until she went to put on her purple Sissuz overall.

"Good party?"

"What?"

"Your brother's birthday party. How did it go?"

"Oh, it was great, thank you. All the uncles and aunts."

"Yes. Sometimes I wish I had a family like that."

"You have a family, don't you?"

He made a face. "My father and mother both died years ago. And to say that I don't get on with my brother is an understatement."

"I'm sorry about that. I suppose I'm lucky, having so many. But it's a nightmare at Christmas, you know, thinking what to buy."

She kept looking at Simon's face, waiting for him to say that when he visited the salon last night the basement was an absolute disaster area, and that she was fired. But all he did was lay his hand on her shoulder and say, "Good luck. And thank you for sweeping up the basement so well."

The front door of the salon opened and Simon's first customer came in: Mrs Edenshaw, who always had her hair washed and blown dry before she went to one of her charity lunches. Simon used so much hairspray on her that she could have safely ridden a motorcycle without a crash helmet.

As Kelly was washing her hair, Kevin said, "Did you see the news this morning? Tragic, wasn't it?"

"We can never watch breakfast TV in our house," said Kelly. "Everybody's making too much noise eating Rice Krispies or shouting downstairs to find out where their best shirt's got to."

"Oh, I thought you would have seen it. Richard Walker was murdered last night."

Kelly stared at him. "Richard Walker the hair stylist? The one that Simon used to work for?"

"That's right. And it's a real Agatha Christie kind of mystery. He was up in his penthouse flat, right on top of his salon in Grosvenor Street, in the middle of the West End. The salon door was locked from the inside. The front door of his flat was locked from the inside. Only one small window was open, in his bathroom, and that was fifteen metres above the next highest rooftop."

"What did Simon say?" asked Kelly. "Was he upset?"

"I don't know," said Susan. "All he did was shrug his shoulders and say something about Gloria."

"He said, *sic transit gloria mundi*," Kevin corrected her. "Thus passes the glory of the world. It's a famous quotation. It's Latin."

"All right, smartyboots. Just because you paid attention at school."

Once she had finished Mrs Edenshaw's hair, Kelly guided her to Simon's station and asked her if she wanted her usual cup of lemon tea. Then, when Simon had started blow-drying her hair, she crossed the salon to the black basement door. For the first time, she noticed that a symbol was painted on it, also in black, but in a matt paint, rather than gloss. It was a cross, upside down, with a circle below it.

She waited until Simon's back was turned and then she opened the door and switched on the light. She looked down the stairs. To her amazement, there was no hair, anywhere. The stairs were clean, the floor was clean. Even the bags had disappeared. No wonder Simon hadn't shouted at her. The basement was immaculate.

She switched off the light and closed the door. She felt as if everything that had happened last night had been a horrible nightmare. The coarse, suggestive voice. The blizzard of hair.

She turned round to find Simon standing right behind her, and jumped.

"Admiring your handiwork?" he asked her.

Kelly nodded, unable to think what to say.

"Well, now that you've finished, perhaps you'd like to wash Miss Steadman. Give her the intensive hair-conditioner. She's got hair like a Brillo pad."

Kelly said, "I heard about Richard Walker. I'm sorry. You used to work for him, didn't you?"

Simon stared at her for a long, long time and didn't blink. "Yes, I'm sorry, too. It's terrible, the bad things that can happen to people these days."

Just before her lunch-break, Ned called her. "Listen – I know it's very short notice, but I was up in Northwood selling some computer systems and I'm only five minutes away from Rayner's Lane and I wondered if you'd like some lunch."

"I, er – I've got some shopping to do."

"Oh, come on. It won't be anything special. Only pizzas. It was so noisy last night that we never really got the chance to talk, did we?"

He met her at Pizza Plaza, a small restaurant at the end of the parade where she worked. They sat at a table in the corner behind a large rubber plant. Ned ordered a four seasons pizza to share between them and half a carafe of white wine. He was very funny and very at ease and he did wonderful impressions of all their uncles and aunts. When he imitated Uncle Sean he held a tomato-shaped ketchup bottle in front of his face to represent his nose.

"Do you know what Uncle Sean said to me? London's so well signposted that you'd have to go an awful long way out of your way to get lost."

While they were eating, he suddenly put down his slice of pizza and said, "I think I'd better come straight out with it. I'd very much like to take you out. You don't have a huge burly boyfriend, do you, who might take exception to that?"

She shook her head. All of a sudden, she felt extremely happy. Outside the restaurant it started to rain, but she didn't mind that at all. Ned reached across and took hold of her hand and squeezed it.

One second he was smiling but the next he lifted his hand away and frowned at it. "Ow. I think I got prickled. Is that a pin you've got in your sleeve, or something?"

Kelly looked down at her wrist. The hairs that she had shaved off yesterday were growing back again, as short, stiff stubble. Not only that, but it looked as if there were more of them, six or seven more.

She blushed in embarrassment and covered her wrist with her other hand. "I don't know what they are. I only noticed them yesterday."

Ned took her hand away and examined her wrist more closely. "You're turning into a werewolf, that's what it is. No – I'm sorry, I didn't mean to upset you. They're unusual, aren't they? I've seen tough hairs like this growing out of a mole. But I've never seen anything like this."

"It's probably nothing. I'll borrow some of Siobhan's depilatory cream."

He looked up into her eyes. "You don't think it's nothing, do you? You're really worried about it. I'm sorry I made fun."

"I don't know. Yes, I am worried about it. Something horrible happened last night and now I've got these on my arm."

He poured her another small glass of wine. "Come on, then, *what* happened last night? You've just agreed to go out with me, haven't you? So if you can't tell your current boyfriend, who can you tell?"

In fragmented bits and pieces, Kelly explained what had happened down in the basement – or rather, what she *thought* had happened down in the basement. "I thought I was going to die. I really did. But this morning, when I took a look, it was all cleaned up, like it had never even happened."

"So – now you're beginning to think that you might have imagined it?"

"Yes. No. If it wasn't for these hairs, I would."

"If you didn't imagine it, who do you think cleared up all of the hair?"

"Well, Simon. Who else could have done it? But he seemed quite sure that it was me."

Ned rubbed the back of his neck, thoughtfully.

"And this voice you heard? You don't know who that might have been, or what they said?"

"It was French, I'm pretty sure of it. But not like the French you used to have at school. They said something like 'bet say lest,' and 'potatoes, potatoes.' But that doesn't make any sense, does it?"

"Was it a man or a woman, do you think?"

Kelly shivered. "I don't know. It was too whispery. It was like somebody trying to tell me something really, really dirty."

Ned took out his pen and made a note on his napkin. "I'll tell you what, I'll go back to work this afternoon and see what I can find on the Internet. You never know, there might be a 'bet say lest' website."

"I'm not making it up, Ned," said Kelly. "And I'm positive that I didn't imagine it."

"I believe you," Ned assured her. "Now look at the time. I need to be getting back to work and so do you."

Ned walked her back along the parade to Sissuz. The rain had eased off and a pale sun the colour of a lemon drop had appeared from behind the clouds. They held hands and their reflections held hands, too, in the upside-down world beneath their feet.

As they passed the TV rental shop, the lunchtime news was appearing on eleven different screens. A body was being carried by paramedics out of a large London building. They couldn't hear the commentary but Kelly could guess who it was: Richard Walker.

"Come on, now," said Ned, pulling her away from the window.

"Yes," she said, and followed him. But for some reason she couldn't stop thinking about Richard Walker and how he might have died.

The story was splashed on the front page of all the afternoon papers: MYSTERY MURDER IN MAYFAIR – Famous hair stylist dies in baffling "locked room" killing.

Kelly and Susan read it during their coffee-break. Richard Walker, thirty-seven, who had cut the hair of several members of the royal family, as well as two of the top girl rock bands and almost every up-and-coming movie star, had been savagely killed in his own bedroom. A spokesman for New Scotland Yard said that the attack was "frenzied, to say the very least".

The police appealed for anybody who might have seen a man in the Grosvenor Square area in the small hours of the morning – a man who must have been "literally drenched in blood".

There were so many unanswered questions: how had the murderer entered Richard Walker's flat? He hadn't come in through the front door, even if he had a key, because the front door was watched twenty-four hours a day by a video camera, and his appearance would have been recorded on tape.

And why would anybody have wanted to kill Richard Walker at all? He was popular, successful –

a great socialite who had no obvious enemies. Was it anything to do with envy, or extortion, or jealousy, or drugs? How had the killer escaped? There were no traces of blood on the bathroom window or the external walls, no signs of a ladder having been erected on the roof.

The police said they had one significant forensic clue, but for the time being they were not going to release any details, for fear of copycat crimes and false confessions.

Simon came into the kitchen while they were reading. "Come on, break's over. Kevin – your four o'clock's here."

"I haven't finished my banana yet."

"Your banana can wait."

Kevin went out into the salon, pushing the entire banana into his mouth so that his cheeks bulged out like a squirrel. But Simon didn't notice him: he had already picked up the newspaper and was scanning the front page story.

Susan and Kelly were about to follow Kevin out, but Kelly suddenly remembered that she needed some more tissues for Susan's station, and turned back to get them. Simon was reading the page headed "Most Brutal Murder I've Ever Seen". And, strangely, he looked as if he were actually smiling.

He looked up when Kelly came back in, and his smile vanished so quickly that she was sure that she was mistaken.

"It's terrible, isn't it?" she said, nodding towards the paper.

"Yes, it is. But you never know what kind of private life he might have been leading. What secrets he had to hide."

"I thought that you and Richard Walker used to be best mates," said Susan.

Simon nodded. "We used to be, Susan. But times change and people change and ambitions change."

"Meaning?"

"Meaning whatever you want it to mean. Now, let's get on with it, shall we? We've got eleven appointments this afternoon and I want you to give your customers the best haircuts they've ever had."

He put his arm around Kelly's shoulders as they left the back room. Kelly glanced up at him and he smiled at her. He had never held her like that before, and never smiled at her like that. She felt unexpectedly breathless. He was, after all, very handsome, even if he was much older than her, and he gave her something else – a feeling that he could protect her, no matter what happened.

Kelly had to sweep up another bagful of hair that evening, and take it down to the basement. She made sure she left the salon door wide open behind her, and with every step she took, she stopped and listened. It was difficult to hear anything, with Simon's hair-dryer whirring and Puff Daddy playing on the music system, but she strained her ears all the same.

Drip, *drip*, *drip* – that was all she heard. Even so, she didn't go all the way down – only as far as the third stair from the bottom. From there, she threw the bag of hair into the corner. It bounced, and rolled over, but by that time she was halfway back up the stairs already.

She was just about to close the door behind her when she thought she heard somebody coughing or laughing. She hesitated, frowning.

"*Bet say lest*," said a thick, phlegmy voice, and it sounded as if it were only centimetres away from her. She slammed the door and locked it.

Simon turned around. "Everything all right?" he asked her. "You look like you've seen a ghost."

She was tempted for a moment to tell him, but he had already turned back to his customer, and was chattering on about his holiday in Ibiza. She picked up an empty shampoo box and carried it out to the back of the salon, and in spite of the fact that she had locked the basement door she still had to look behind to make sure that nothing was following her.

While she was tidying the stockroom, Mrs Marshall came downstairs, with two of her cats dangling under her arms. Mrs Marshall had wild white hair which she attempted to pin up into a bun with scores of grips and slides and combs, a withered, sunken face and startling eyes that revolved as she talked. She was wearing a frayed, Japanese silk dressing-gown over a grubby white Woolworth's jumper and a pair of baggy green tracksuit bottoms. A cigarette hung from the corner of her mouth.

"Oh, it's *you*, Kelly love! 'Ow are you? 'Ow did yer little brother's party go? Nobody sick, was they? That's what my boys always did, when I gave them birthday parties. Too much cake, too much pop, and *blurrk*, up it all came. Mind you, they're a bit older now. Fifty-one and forty-nine. Kids of their own."

Her cats struggled free and dropped on to the floor. She opened the back door into the concrete yard outside. "Go on," she chided them. "Go and do your business. And no flirting with that tom next door."

Kelly said, "I love that black cat. What's his name?"

"It's not an 'e, it's a she. 'Er name's Isabel."

"She's beautiful."

"Oh, not just beautiful. She's my watch-cat. She looks after me, Isabel does. She's my eyes and ears. She hears anybody coming up the stairs, you should see 'er tail standing up. And she can always tell good people from bad. You take that boss of yours, that Simon Crane. She only 'as to take one look at 'im and 'er 'ackles rise."

"Simon's all right. He's great to work with."

"Well, you might think he's all right, but you

know ’e’s been trying to get me out of my flat, don’t you?”

“I didn’t, no. What does he want to do that for?”

“’E’s got plans, that’s why. ’E wants to turn my flat into some sort of lifestyle centre, that’s what ’e calls it. You know, all them exercise machines and saunas and that.”

“But he can’t just turn you out, can he?”

Mrs Marshall coughed and shook her head. “No, love, ’e can’t. I’m a sitting tenant and nobody can throw me out. That’s why he lost ’is rag the last time he come upstairs to talk to me. ’E offered me twenty-five thousand pounds to get out, but I wasn’t ’aving it. This is my ’ome and this is where I’m going to stay.”

Isabel came back through the door. She lifted her head and sniffed at Kelly suspiciously. Kelly bent down and made little kissing noises to encourage her to come closer. “She’s gorgeous, aren’t you, Isabel? What a beautiful girl!”

Kelly picked her up and stroked her head. But Isabel suddenly twisted herself around, and yowled. She scrabbled her claws and jumped out of Kelly’s arms and fled upstairs.

“Well, *that* wasn’t very polite, was it?” said Mrs Marshall. “I wonder what got into ’er, all of a sudden? She ’asn’t ’urt you, ’as she?”

“I don’t think so,” said Kelly, pushing back the sleeve of her Sissuz overall. She was disconcerted to see that the hairs on her wrist had grown even more. They were thicker, too.

She held out her wrist to Mrs Marshall and said, "What do you think these are? These hairs? I'm a bit worried about them."

Mrs Marshall took her cigarette out of her mouth and peered at them. "Blessed if I know. They're probably something to do with your 'ormones. I knew a girl at school and she 'ad a moustache that would have looked good on a guardsman."

"I don't know... I shave them off with my dad's razor but they keep on growing back."

"Well, if they bother you that much, you should go to see your doctor. He can give you what's-its-name to get rid of them. Electrocution."

Just then, Simon came out of the salon. "Kelly! I really need you in here! Come on, you've got too much to do to spend your time gossiping to obstinate old cows."

"'Ere!" Mrs Marshall retorted. "'Oo are you calling an obstinate old cow?"

"You," said Simon. "I'm trying to build up a first-class business here and you're the only person standing in my way."

Mrs Marshall gathered up her other cat under her arm like a handbag. "You mark my words, something 'orrible is going to 'appen to you one day. Something really, really 'orrible."

"It has already," said Simon. "And it's you."

As they went back into the salon, Kelly said, "You shouldn't be so mean to her. Poor old thing. All she's got are those cats."

"You're probably right," Simon agreed. "But if she happened to die tomorrow – well, let me put it this way, I wouldn't exactly be stricken with grief."

When Kelly came out of work that evening she was pleasantly surprised to find that Ned was waiting for her in his white Ford Escort. He wound down the window and called out, "Wanna lift, darling?"

"I might," she teased him. She climbed into the car and he started up the engine. "Actually," she said, "it's only ten minutes' walk."

He pulled out into the traffic. "I know. But I wanted to see you. I've been surfing the net."

"And?"

"Nothing. Not a sausage. No 'bet say lest'. Nothing about potatoes. Well, plenty about King Edwards and Maris Pipers and how to make Cheddar'n'potato bake, but nothing that would frighten you. I really need more to go on."

"It happened again today. It went down to the basement and somebody said 'bet say lest'. It was horrible. It sounded so close. It was like I could almost feel them breathing on me."

Ned turned left into Waverley Road. "I think I ought to come down and take a look at this basement of yours. Maybe there's a squatter hiding in it."

"How can there be? How could he get in and out? There's always somebody in the salon during the day, and at night we always lock up and put the alarm on. Besides, there's no food down there, or anything like that. No blankets."

"There's hair. That's warm."

"I know. But I don't think it's a squatter. I don't see how it could be."

"All the same, I'd like to have look around. I just need a clue, that's all."

They reached Kelly's house. Ned said, "Listen, how about I come around later and take you out to the Harvest Moon? They've got an Irish band playing this evening. It'll take your mind off all of this basement business."

"All right," said Kelly, "I'd like that. I should have finished my supper by eight."

She put her hand down to release her seat-belt buckle, but as she did so he put his hand over it, and stopped her. "How about a kiss before I let you go?"

With her free hand she brushed the hair away

from her forehead. "You think a lot of yourself, don't you?"

"Oh, yes. I'm brimming with confidence. Everybody says that."

She gave him a quick peck on the cheek. "That's all for now," she said, and climbed out of the car with a mischievous laugh. He pulled an exaggeratedly sad face, and drove off, tooting his horn. As she stood on the pavement watching him drive away, she couldn't stop herself from smiling.

Until she reached down and rubbed the stiff, prickly hairs on her wrist, thicker than ever.

Her first customer the next morning was Miss Paleforth. Kelly rather liked Miss Paleforth, but Kevin and Susan thought she was hopelessly eccentric.

"I never know what to say to her," Kevin complained. "If you ask her things like, 'Where are you going on your holidays this year?' she just looks at you as if she doesn't know what the word 'holidays' means."

Miss Paleforth came in once a week, not always on the same day, to have her long blonde hair washed and curled. She couldn't have been more than twenty-nine or thirty years old, yet she wore faded velvet dresses that hung down to her ankles, and granny shawls, and black elastic-sided boots; and her foundation was so pale and luminous that it made her face shine silver, like the moon. She was almost beautiful, in an odd, unworldly way. She had full, curving lips, which she always painted with lavender lip-colour.

As Kelly started to wash her hair, Miss Paleforth suddenly said, "There's something different about you today. What is it?"

"You'll tell me if this water's too hot?" said Kelly.

"I'll scream like a banshee. But you haven't answered my question. There's something different about you. Your aura. I'm very sensitive to auras, you know, and yours is very disturbed. A young girl like you, your aura should be bright and glowing. Yours is all stirred up like the bottom of a muddy pond.

She narrowed her eyes and peered at Kelly intently. "A muddy pond with something *dark* swimming in it. Something very, *very* dark."

Kelly tried to smile, but she found it difficult. "I'm just a little bit worried, that's all."

"It's not boyfriend trouble, is it? No, it's much darker than that. You feel threatened. Even more than that, you feel anxious about your physical health."

Kelly hesitated for a moment, but then she said, "Actually, it's this," and showed Miss Paleforth the back of her wrist. Miss Paleforth held her arm very gently and stroked the hairs with one of her silver-ringed fingers.

"I haven't seen anything like this for years and years," she said. She tried to tug out one of the hairs, but it was so firmly rooted that she couldn't.

"What is it?" asked Kelly.

"In magical circles, they call it devil's hair."

"Devil's hair? What's that?"

"Devil's hair grows on you when you've come into contact with somebody irredeemably evil. Somebody so black-hearted that even hell wouldn't have them. Can you think who that might have been?"

Kelly shook her head. "I've never met anybody *evil.*" She was beginning to think that Miss Paleforth was even more eccentric than she had first supposed. Potty, even. She tried to take her hand away but Miss Paleforth gripped it tighter.

"You should come and see me after work. Look – I'll give you my number."

"I can't," said Kelly. "I'm going to see the doctor tonight."

"You mark my words, no doctor in the world can get rid of the devil's hair. But, go if you feel you have to. So long as you don't forget to come back to see me when everything else has failed."

She rummaged in her knitted brown Indian bag and produced a shopping list. She wrote her phone number on the back, in eyebrow pencil. "Thank you," said Kelly, dubiously.

"Listen," Miss Paleforth insisted, "I know you don't believe me. I know you think that I'm cracked. But you could be in very great danger. This evil person could still be close to you. Whoever it is, they could still be a terrible threat. The devil's hair will always grow thicker and faster, and if you don't get rid of it, it could completely overwhelm you.

"You could turn into something evil, too. Something so evil that you can't even begin to imagine it."

Simon came over and asked, "Everything all right here, Kelly?"

Miss Paleforth gave him a wide, disarming smile. "Kelly's the best new assistant you've ever had, Simon. You should double her wages."

"I don't know about that," Simon laughed. "Perhaps I'll give her five minutes longer for her lunch-break."

He turned away – and as he did so, for just a split second, Kelly caught Miss Paleforth staring at him with her eyes so wide that it was almost frightening, the way that a cat stares at a snarling dog. Kelly felt a sharp tingle of alarm. *Surely she doesn't think that this "devil's hair" is anything to do with him*, she thought. If there was somebody evil at this salon, it couldn't be him. The way he had put his arm around her had given her the feeling that he really cared for her.

She gave Miss Paleforth some herbal conditioner and roughly towelled her hair. Then she took her over to Susan's station to be trimmed and dried. As she left her, Miss Paleforth caught hold of her sleeve and said, "Don't forget, Kelly. You can come and see me any time of the day or night. Don't be afraid. You're not alone. If you need me, I'll always be here to help you."

"What was she on about?" asked Kevin, as Kelly rinsed out the basins.

"I don't know. She's quite scary. It wouldn't surprise me if she's a witch or something."

"What do you mean?"

Reluctantly, Kelly said, "I've grown these hairs on my arm."

"Hairs? Show me."

Kelly pulled up her sleeve and showed him. He wrinkled up his nose and said, "That's peculiar, isn't it? But nothing a pair of scissors wouldn't sort out."

"You think so? Miss Paleforth said that this was devil's hair, and it's grown on me because I've been close to somebody really, really evil."

That lunchtime, she went along to the surgery on the Harrow Road and saw Dr Cummings. He was a young doctor with hair that sprigged up at the back, and bright red cheeks. He examined the back of Kelly's wrist and then he peered at the hairs through a magnifying glass.

"This is *very* odd, isn't it?" he said. "They're all different colours."

"I've tried shaving them off but they always grow back; and they seem to grow quicker every time."

"I think the answer is going to be electrolysis, to remove the roots altogether. I can put you on to a trichologist at the Middlesex Hospital."

"Why do you think they suddenly started growing

like that?" asked Kelly. "I'm not going to grow any more, am I? I mean, it looks as if they're spreading."

Dr Cummings sat back in his chair. "I don't think you're going to end up as Kelly the bearded lady, so don't worry about that. It's probably nothing more than a minor imbalance in your hair follicles."

He wrote her a note for the hospital. He gave her a reassuring pat on the back as she left the surgery, but when she looked up at him she realized that he didn't know anything more about what was happening to her than she did. She began to feel as if the ground was gradually dissolving beneath her feet.

Kevin gave her a Bounty bar as soon as she came back to the salon, so that he wouldn't feel so guilty about eating two of them himself. "Simon's gone off for the rest of the day. Something to do with his lifestyle centre. I don't know, he seems to be getting all stressed about it. Just because old Mrs Marshall won't leave."

Kelly moved the chairs back and swept underneath them. "You should have heard what he said to her yesterday. He called her an old cow, right to her face."

"That's awful! An insult to elderly cattle everywhere!"

"What time's your next appointment? You were going to show me how to do a scalp treatment."

"Not till three-thirty. Did you hear the latest

about Richard Walker? It was on the news this morning."

"I didn't have time," said Kelly. She pushed all the hair-cuttings into the middle of the floor and went to fetch the dustpan.

"The police say that he was being blackmailed. They don't know who the blackmailer was, but apparently it had been going on for years."

"What was he being blackmailed about?"

"Well, it was weird. One of his regular customers used to be Chrissy Black – you know, the model who used to do all of those chocolate commercials. One of his top stylists fell in love with her, really badly. He took her out for a while, but then she dumped him. But the next time she went to Richard Walker's salon for a haircut, this stylist went up to her and chopped half of her hair off. You remember what gorgeous hair she had."

"You're joking! What did she do?"

"Well, she had to wear wigs for about six months. But she agreed to keep quiet about it in return for a hundred thousand pounds in compensation – and, of course, the stylist himself agreed to keep quiet about it, in case he never worked again. If the press had got hold of the story, Richard Walker would have been ruined.

"But it seems that somebody else knew what had happened, and that person threatened to go to the *News of the World* unless Richard Walker paid him not to – and kept on paying him. But they said on the news this morning that Richard Walker finally got fed up with paying out so much money and told a friend that he was going to go to the police and make a complaint, no matter what it did to his reputation. Except that he never went."

"So they think the blackmailer murdered him?"

"That's what it looks like."

"That's awful!"

"I know. But the trouble is, the police still can't work out how the murderer got in there. And there are no clues in Richard Walker's flat. His desk was forced open and all of his papers were taken. So even if he *did* have a record of who was blackmailing him, it's gone."

That afternoon, with Simon away, the atmosphere in the salon was very relaxed. Susan put the music up louder, and Kevin entertained them all by dancing a one-man salsa while he was backcombing Mrs Bartlett's mock-ginger hair. Kevin was very good with his older ladies. He always knew how to flatter them and even when they asked to have their hair tinted purple he didn't raise an eyebrow. "Purple, Mrs McAllister? It's so *you*!"

Susan's client was a pretty young Punjabi girl. Susan had a flair for cutting hair so that it could be worn straight and modest (so that fathers didn't complain) and pinned up for parties and discos. She was also brilliant with Afro-Caribbean curls and she had created her own trademark style which was a mixture of waves and dreads.

"I think Simon's problem is that he's too ambitious. He wants to be Nicky Clarke, you know, but he wants it all to happen *tomorrow*. He's very, very good; but he doesn't realize that it takes years to build up a business like that."

Susan picked up a jar of conditioner and tried to open it. "I wish they wouldn't screw the lids on so tight. Kevin ... can you open this for me?"

Kevin took it and wrestled with it until he was gasping and red in the face, but he couldn't open it, either. He handed it to Kelly and said, "The thing to do is run it under hot water."

Kelly took it over to the backwash basins, but before she turned on the water she gave the lid a twist herself. She used her left hand, which had always been her weaker hand and which now had the hairs growing out of it. And the lid came off easily, as if it hadn't been tightened at all. She held it up and said, "Ta-*daaa*!"

"Oh come on, I must have loosened it for you," said Kevin.

"No, you didn't," Susan teased him. "You're the puniest man in the world and you just don't want to admit it."

"I'm not puny," Kevin protested. "I'm sensitive, but I'm strong."

Kelly screwed the lid back on the jar as tight as she could and said, "Go on, then. Open it now."

Kevin tried, grunting and straining, but he couldn't. In the end he had to hand it back to Kelly, who opened it with no trouble at all.

"You've been working out," Kevin accused her.

"Of course she hasn't," said Susan. "Look at those skinny arms!"

"All right, then – arm-wrestle," said Kevin.

"Kevin, what about Mrs Bartlett?"

"Oh, don't you mind me," said Mrs Bartlett, turning around in her chair. "I always enjoy a bit of fun and games."

Kevin went over to the counter, rolled up his sleeve, and held up his arm. "Come on then, let's see how strong you really are!"

Reluctantly, Kelly walked up to the counter, propped her left elbow on it, and grasped Kevin's left hand.

"Ready…" said Susan. "Go!"

Kelly gripped Kevin's hand as tight as she could. It was incredible. She could feel the muscles in his fingers. She could feel his tendons. She could even feel his *bones*. She gripped him tighter and tighter and as she did so she looked into his eyes. He was staring at her, his mouth puckered with effort, and there were beads of sweat trickling down his cheeks.

"Come on, Kevin!" Susan urged him. "She's only a girl!"

Kevin started to make a hissing sound between his teeth. His arm began to tremble. His whole body began to tremble. Centimetre by quivering centimetre, Kelly forced his hand sideways. She felt as if she could have won this bout with one quick push, but she wanted him to feel that he had put up a fight. With four brothers, she knew a lot about masculine pride – and while she was quite prepared to beat Kevin, if she could, she didn't want to humiliate him.

Kevin grunted, "*Gragghhh!*" and pushed harder and harder; but Kelly squeezed his hand even tighter. She heard his finger-joints crackle, and she suddenly understood that she was more than strong enough to crush his hand like a run-over pigeon.

Kevin shouted, "*Aaaaahhhhh!*" and it was then that Kelly let go, immediately, and stepped away from the counter, with both hands raised.

"I'm sorry! I'm so sorry! I didn't mean to hurt you!"

Kevin flapped his hand in the air and blew on his fingers. "I'll tell you one thing," he said. "You won't need any nutcrackers at Christmas. You'll be able to do it with your bare hands!"

Susan was laughing, and even Mrs Bartlett was clapping. "Good for you, girl! Good for you!" But then Susan caught the look on Kelly's face and she stopped laughing, and came up to her, and laid a hand on her shoulder. "What's wrong?" she asked. "You beat him, didn't you?"

"Look at me," said Kelly, and there were tears in her eyes. "Do I look like the kind of girl who could beat any man at anything at all?"

Susan didn't answer. She didn't know what to say. Kevin went back to Mrs Bartlett and after a while, she went back to her client, too.

Kelly went into the storeroom at the back of the salon and half-closed the door. She looked at herself in the mirror next to the shelves full of clean towels. It was an old mirror, measled and discoloured, and it made her appear older than she really was. Almost like an elderly woman.

"What's happening to me?" she asked herself.

She lifted her left arm. She had shaved off the hairs again, but already she could feel them beginning to grow back, prickly and coarse. She flexed her fingers, and she felt incredibly strong, as if she could crush anything – not just Kevin's fingers, but anything at all.

There was an old green enamel mug on the shelf, into which they each dropped fifty pence every week to cover the cost of tea and coffee. She picked it up in her right hand and squeezed it, but she couldn't make any impression at all. But then she transferred it to her left hand, and squeezed it again, and the mug crumpled and bent until it was almost bent double.

She put the mug back on the shelf and she was

shaking. She leaned back against the wall and whispered, "*What's happening to me*?"

After a minute or two, Susan opened the door. "Are you all right, Kelly? You look ever so washed out. You don't want to go home, do you?"

"I'm OK. I'm grand. Just give me a moment, will you please? I'll be back out directly."

When Susan had gone, Kelly went to the phone and punched out Ned's number.

"Ned McGee here. What can I do for you?"

"Ned, it's me, Kelly. I need your help."

"Are you all right, Kelly? You sound terrible."

Tears were running down Kelly's cheeks already. "I need somebody to help me, Ned. I don't understand what's happening to me. I need you to come down here and look at the basement. I'm sure there's something down there. I don't know what it is, but it's changing me. It's making me different. I've got these hairs on my hand and I've just crushed a mug and I've arm-wrestled Kevin and I don't know what to do."

"You crushed a mug and you arm-wrestled? I don't know what you're talking about."

"It's my *hand*, Ned! It's doing things that I don't want it to do!"

"Listen, don't get upset. I'll come round and pick you up as soon as I can. I'm in Uxbridge at the moment but I could get there by six."

"That's all right. We're closing early today,

because Simon's not here. But you will come, won't you?"

"Of course I'll come. I promise you. Now don't panic. Don't get hysterical. I'll go down into that basement for you and if there's anything there, I'll find it, and get rid of it. I promise."

"All right," said Kelly, wiping her eyes.

She put down the phone. She spent nearly a minute composing herself, blowing her nose and blinking. Then she took three deep breaths to steady herself and went back into the salon. "Anybody want coffee?" she asked, trying to sound bright. "Mrs Bartlett? How about some tea?"

Susan packed up her scissors and combs and said, "Why don't you come back to my house this evening? My mum's dying to see you again, and it's meat patties tonight. And my mum's meat patties ... *mmm*! I always eat three too many!"

Kelly shook her head. "Thanks for asking. But I think I'll stay here for a while and tidy everything up for the morning. Ned's coming around later."

Susan said, "You really like that Ned, don't you?"

Kelly blushed; but at that moment Kevin gave her a wave from the back door, and called out, "G'night, Crusher."

"Goodnight, Kev. Sorry about your hand."

"That's all right. I never wanted to be a concert pianist anyway."

After they had left, Kelly sat in one of the chairs and spun herself around a few times. Then, edgy and bored, she put a Spice Girls CD on the salon's music system and started to dance to it, watching herself in the mirror. She imagined herself at Wembley Stadium, in front of an audience of thousands of cheering and screaming fans. She danced to the left; she danced to the right; she twirled herself around.

It was while she was twirling herself around, however, that she saw somebody peering into the salon window. A hunched figure, in a black coat with the collar turned up and a large black hat, with the whitest of faces and a grin like a crack in a plaster wall. She stopped twirling at once, and almost lost her balance. The figure grinned at her even more broadly and walked off along the street, with a strange swaying gait. It was only a homeless old man who used to hang around the parade in the evenings, but all the same he left the skin on the back of Kelly's neck crawling with fright.

She listened to the CD a little longer, but the old man's unexpected appearance had badly shaken her, and she couldn't stop glancing towards the basement door. She knew it was locked – she had turned the key herself. But after her last experience down there, she wasn't sure *what* could happen. And if Miss Paleforth was right, she had touched somebody or something down amongst those bags of hair that was evil itself.

She thought she heard a knocking, bumping sound in the basement, although she couldn't be sure. She immediately went over to the CD system and switched it off, and listened, but she didn't hear it again. There was no chance that she was going to open the basement door to see if there was anything down there – not until Ned came, anyway.

She had been down there only twice today, to get rid of rubbish, and both times she had run back up the stairs as fast as she could. But she hadn't heard anything. No rustlings, no whisperings, no hideous dragging noises.

She was still listening when the doorbell shrilled, and made her jump. She went to the back door and opened it, and there to her relief was Ned, wearing a brown leather jacket and a wide smile.

"Hey, how are you?" he said, giving her a kiss on the cheek. "I got here as quick as I could; but you know what the traffic's like at this time of night. Murder!"

He took hold of Kelly's hand and gave it a reassuring squeeze. "Are you OK?" he asked her. "You're looking a bit pale, if you don't mind my saying so."

"I'm all right now that you're here."

Ned walked into the salon and took a look around. "Nice bright place to work," he remarked.

"Except for *that*," said Kelly, nodding towards the basement door.

Ned approached it and turned the handle.

"I locked it. I don't know if there's anybody down there or not, but I wasn't going to take any chances. Not while I was alone." She told him what Miss Paleforth had said to her about the devil's hair.

"For goodness' sake, I wouldn't worry about *her*. She sounds like some nutty woman trying to put the fear of God into you, that's all."

"She scared me, though. She really, really scared me."

Ned saw the upside-down cross on top of the door, and touched it with his fingertips. "This is weird, isn't it? You wouldn't normally expect to see something like this in a hairdresser's salon. It's an *ankh*."

"What's that?"

"It's an Egyptian good-luck charm. I know that because my sister wears one. She's still a bit of a hippie, you know. Peace and love and incense, that sort of thing. But this *ankh* is upside down, isn't it? What do you think that means?"

"*Bad* luck?" Kelly suggested.

"Let's hope not. Anyway … let's take a look at this basement of yours. If there's anybody here, we'll find them."

Kelly caught hold of his hand. "Ned – perhaps we shouldn't do this."

"Of course we should. You should always face up to the things that frighten you the most. And what could this be, down in the basement, when you think about it logically? At the very worst, it's some poor old squatter who can't find anywhere else to go."

"Well, all right then," said Kelly, and she turned the key in the basement door. "The light's on the right … that's it, a little bit higher."

Ned switched on the light. He peered into the basement and made a show of cupping his hand around his ear, listening. "I don't see anything, and I don't hear anything, either." He sniffed. "It smells a bit musty, that's all."

He went down the stairs, with Kelly reluctantly following him. "Hello?" he called out. "Is there anybody here? If there is, we're not going to hurt you. We just want to talk."

Nobody answered. All they could hear was the muffled traffic outside, and the sound of footsteps, and the constant dripping from the leaky pipe.

Ned prodded one of the bags of hair with his foot. "This is where you keep all the sweepings from the salon?"

"Yes, until the dustmen call on Tuesday and Thursday mornings. We can't leave the bags outside because Mrs Marshall's cats tear them open and there's hair all over the place. It's a health risk."

Ned approached the bags of hair and gently prodded at one of them with his finger. "When you came down here, one of these burst, right? And this whole basement was filled up with a storm of hair?"

"That's right," Kelly nodded. "I almost suffocated."

Ned strained his eyes to see into the darkness beyond the alcove. "You don't think that anybody's hiding in there, do you?"

"I don't know. I don't think so."

"I mean, there's no smell of food; no old newspapers; no garbage. If somebody were living down here, we'd be able to smell them."

Ned took out a penknife and cut open one of the bags that had been recently stacked on top of the pile. A glittering cascade of hair fell out, of every conceivable colour. Ned sifted his hand through it, and let it fall from his fingers. "There..." he said. "Look at it ... that was somebody's crowning glory. But that's all."

Kelly wrinkled her nose up. "I can't stand it. By the time I get home in the evening I feel that my lungs must be full of it."

"Oh, come on with you, it's only hair," said Ned. He prodded another bag, and another. They listened, but there was no whispering, no frightening innuendos, no filthy French gobbledygook.

Ned climbed over the bags, his feet slipping, until he had to crawl on his hands and knees. He made his way right to the back of the basement, to the darkened alcove, and stuck his head into it, and looked around, Kelly waited on the bottom stair, anxiously clutching the rail.

"There's nothing here, as far as I can make out,"

Ned called back. "A couple of broken chairs and some old-fashioned hair-dryers. That's all. There's nobody living here, and that's for sure."

He clambered back again. "I don't know what it is you thought you heard here, Kelly; or what you thought you saw, but it certainly isn't here now."

"I didn't imagine it," Kelly protested. "There was something here. *Somebody* here. I heard them whispering and laughing – and you only have to look at my wrist."

"I know that, sweetheart," said Ned. "But sometimes – you know – your mind can play tricks on you. It really can. In winter, when I had to walk back home from school in the dark, I was always sure that this shadowy monster was following me. I used to walk faster and faster and then I used to start running and by the time I reached home I was in a total panic, and my ma never understood why. But *I* did. To me, that shadowy monster was completely real, and I was always sure that it was going to catch up with me one day, and carry me off."

"You're not making me feel any better," said Kelly, still looking nervously around the basement.

"I'm sorry. But I don't think there's anything here. I really don't."

Kelly started to climb back up the stairs. As she did so, she heard a very soft rustling sound. She turned back, and saw that the hair from the bag which Ned had split open was sliding down the bags below it, on to the floor. But it wasn't just a cascade of loose hair. It had twined itself together somehow, and formed a long snake-like shape – an almost-endless python of shining, glistening hair.

"*Ned*," she whispered. "Look at that."

The hair continued to pour down on to the floor. It even seemed to have a rearing head of its own, exactly like a snake; and when it reached the concrete it started to flow swiftly across it, straight towards the stairs. Even as its head twined itself around the banister post, the rest of its body was still pouring out of the broken bag. It must have been ten metres long, and it was still growing, and it was still coming after them.

They stared at it for one horrified split second; and even in that one split second the hair-snake had managed to flow up another two stairs. It made a soft, relentless hissing sound, like steam escaping.

Kelly screamed, "What is it? Ned – what is it?"

But Ned didn't answer. He pushed her forcefully up the stairs until they had reached the salon door. It was only then that he shouted, "*Go*! Get out of here! Quick!"

She stumbled into the salon. Ned followed her out of the door and turned around to shut it. But as he did so, the hair-snake came rearing up the staircase and lunged at him. It even had a thin, predatory mouth, and fangs formed out of human hair, all bonded together so that they shone as sharp and as venomous as a real snake's teeth. Kelly pushed Ned's shoulder and the hair-snake missed him by less than three centimetres. Instantly, it arched itself back up again, in the middle of the doorway, ready for a second strike.

Kelly snatched up the broom which was leaning against Simon's station, and wildly struck out at the hair-snake, hitting it one way, and then the other. It felt as strong and wiry as a real snake, and each time she hit it, it grew more and more furious, lashing out at her with its forked tongue flickering.

"*Kelly*!" shouted Ned. "*Hit it again*! *Now*!"

She hit it, but the hair-snake was so powerful that it knocked the broom out of her hands and sent it clattering across the floor.

"Don't move!" Ned warned her. "Don't make a sound!"

"What?" panted Kelly. The hair-snake was slowly lifting its head right up into the air, right over her. It swayed from side to side, as if it were blindly trying to decide where she was. She stood as still as she could, and tried to suppress her breathing. The hair-snake's head swung dangerously close to her face, and she couldn't help shrinking back from it, but Ned waved his hand to her to tell her not to move a muscle.

Seconds crawled past, although they felt like hours. Then – without warning – the hair-snake lashed its head wildly from side to side. Kelly screamed and stepped backwards, tripping over Simon's chair. The hair-snake immediately stiffened, and whipped its head back, all ready to strike.

"*Ned*!" Kelly screamed, trying to disentangle herself from Simon's chair. The hair-snake lunged at her, but as it did so, Ned threw himself forward like a rugby player and collided with the open cellar door, slamming it shut. Instantly, the hair-snake's head was chopped off, and it dropped on to the salon floor as nothing more than a few clumps of mixed human hair.

Kelly slowly climbed to her feet, and she was shaking. Ned came over and put his arm around her and held her tight. "It's all right, now," he reassured her. "It's dead, whatever it is."

All the same, they approached the hair with the utmost caution. Kelly had a horrible dread that the scattered hair would suddenly reassemble itself into the shape of a snake's head, and take a bite at her. But Ned gave it a contemptuous kick, so that it was thrown in all directions.

"Did you see that?" he asked Kelly. "It was a snake, wasn't it? You and I, we both saw it, didn't we? But it's just hair, that's all. Nothing but hair."

"I can't believe it. It came after us so quickly. And it was so *strong*."

Ned ran his hand through his hair. "I don't know. I don't understand it. I've never seen anything like that in my life."

"What about the rest of it, I wonder?" asked

Kelly. "Do you think it's still there, behind the door? I hope it's not like one of those worms – you know, when you cut them in half the two halves still go wriggling off on their own."

"Well, there's only one way to find out," said Ned. He let go of her, and put his hand on the doorknob and started to turn it. "Don't," said Kelly. "*Please* don't. I'm scared."

Ned said, "Listen, Kelly. Something's happening here at Sissuz that's frightening the life out of you. What are you going to do? Run away from it? Give up your job?"

"You saw that snake as clearly as I did."

"Of course I did. But there must be some kind of explanation. I don't believe in ghosts and werewolves, and I don't believe in snakes made out of hair. Well, I do. But maybe it's some kind of a trick, you know, like the Indian rope-trick."

Kelly stared at the door handle and anxiously bit her lip. "All right, then," she said. "But I'm going to stand over here by the basins."

"Fair enough," said Ned. Very slowly, he opened the door. Only a few centimetres at first, in case the rest of the hair-snake was waiting to lunge at them. Then – when nothing happened – he opened it a little wider, and then a little more. Finally, he swung it right back.

There was nothing there. Only the stairs, without a single hair on them. The hair-snake had vanished as quickly as it had first appeared. Ned shaded his eyes against the naked light bulb and peered down the stairs. He gave Kelly the thumbs-up. "It's gone," he told her. "And by the looks of it, the hair's all back in the bag."

Kelly came across and took a look for herself. The hair-snake had completely gone. No wonder Simon had thought that she swept up so well the other night. The hair had a life of its own, it was *alive*, and it could slide back into its bags whenever it wanted to.

"What do we do now?" she asked Ned.

"Go and have a drink," said Ned, emphatically.

"But we have to tell somebody! We have to tell Simon, or even the police! We could have been killed!"

"What are we going to tell the police? They'll only think that we're pulling their legs. I mean, would *you* believe anybody who said they'd been chased by a huge great snake made out of people's hair-clippings?"

"I suppose not. But what about Simon?"

"I don't know. I think we'd be wiser not to tell anybody anything – not until we find out what's really happening here. We don't want to be making complete fools of ourselves, do we?"

"But I'm sure Simon would help."

"I expect you're probably right. But just ask yourself this: who painted that *ankh* over the door there, and why?"

"I don't know, but—"

Ned put his fingers to his lips. "Let's just keep this quiet for a while. As my old grandfather used to say, 'A second's silence can save you a lifetime of trouble.' "

"What does that mean?"

"I'm not entirely sure. But I think we'd be doing ourselves a favour if we kept this snake to ourselves."

That night, Kelly dreamed that she was in Egypt. The buildings all around her were dazzlingly white – so bright and blurry that she could hardly look at them. She heard pan-pipes and the insistent *tap*, *tap*, *tapping* of a hardskinned drum.

She came out of the shadows into a square, where a man in a fez and a long white robe was sitting cross-legged – except that he wasn't sitting on the ground, he was floating five or ten centimetres above it.

"*Salaam*," he said, and gave her a secretive smile. Then he picked up his pipes again and began to play, a throaty, suggestive song that spoke to her of warm nights out on the desert, with the stars clustering themselves into mysterious constellations; and of floating down the Nile, wearing nothing but a gauzy dress, with the Sphinx gazing down at her as if it were thinking of pouncing.

In the square, a woven basket opened. Its lid dropped off, and rocked on the ground, and a snake rose out of it, like a flat-headed cobra. Only when she looked at it again, it wasn't a cobra at all. It was a human hand, forming the shape of a cobra.

She couldn't move. She couldn't run away. She knew that the alleyways in the *souk* behind her were a maze, from which she would never be able to escape. She remained paralysed while the human hand slid out of the basket, followed by a long, pale arm – as long as a snake, or longer – sliding its way towards her over the paving-blocks and finally rearing up in front of her.

I can't move, she thought to herself, panicking. *I can't protect myself. I'm so frightened that I want to scream but my throat muscles won't work.*

The hand-cobra swayed in front of her. It hesitated for a while. Whenever she moved her head to the left, it followed her. Whenever she moved her head to the right, it did the same. She was thinking about throwing herself backwards, and running away, when the hand-cobra suddenly darted towards her and grabbed her by the throat.

She tried to shout out, but it was squeezing her larynx too tightly. She tried to pull it away, but it was gripping her so fiercely that she felt as if it were draining her of all her energy, all her strength. Her breathing became one high-pitched whistle after another, like the pan-pipes. She saw prickly stars, and swimming scarlet circles, and waves of mauve like an ocean in a watercolour painting.

If all the world were apple pie, she thought to herself. It was a silly poem that her mother used to tell her when she was small, but she was trying to think of something real, something reassuring. *And all the sea were ink.*

Her brain was filling up with blackness. She couldn't breathe. She couldn't breathe and she didn't know why.

And all the trees
Were bread and cheese…

She suddenly opened her eyes and she wasn't sleeping, she was wide awake. She wasn't in Egypt, she was lying on the top bunkbed in the back bedroom of Waverley Road and she was gripping her throat with her own left hand, strangling herself.

She tried to scream, but she couldn't. She gargled and choked and kicked her legs but she was all tangled up in her duvet and her hand just wouldn't let go.

The bedroom light blinked on, and she was dazzled. She heard Siobhan shouting, "Kelly! *Kelly*! For goodness' sake, Kelly, what's the matter with you?"

Kelly's hand gripped her throat harder and harder and all she could see was a scarlet fog. But then she felt Siobhan wrestling her hand away, and holding it tight, and gradually the room came back into focus, and Siobhan appeared, like a face suddenly coming through a parted net curtain, her hair all tousled, and looking so worried. "Kelly, wake up! Kelly, listen to me! Kelly, wake up!"

Kelly blinked at her. "Siobhan – what's happening? What time is it?"

"Two-thirty. You were screaming in your sleep. Dear God, girl, you were trying to strangle yourself!"

Kelly propped herself up on one elbow. Leonardo di Caprio beamed at her from across the room and she decided then and there that he looked much too smug and podgy for her: she would rather have Ned. "I had a nightmare," she said.

"We all have nightmares, darling. But we don't all try to strangle ourselves."

Kelly looked down at her left hand. It didn't feel like her own hand any more. She recognized the silver braided ring that her grandmother had given her, and she recognized her lifeline and her heartline and her headline, but it still didn't feel like hers.

She turned her hand over. On the back of her wrist, the hairs had not only grown longer and wirier, they had started to weave themselves together.

Siobhan said, "Are you all right now? I have to get up really early in the morning."

Kelly coughed. "I think so. I'll just get myself a glass of water, that's all."

She padded along to the bathroom in her long candy-striped nightshirt. She opened the medicine cabinet and took out her father's razor. In the mirror she thought she looked pale and haggard, with purple circles under her eyes. She rubbed the back of her hand with soap, and started to shave the hairs off her wrist. But then she stopped. A dark, commanding force inside her head was telling her that she shouldn't – that she *couldn't*. She tried again, but every time she brought the razor close to the hairs, her hand veered away.

It was then, for the first time, that she wondered if she was going to die.

Simon allowed her the morning off for her appointment at the trichology department at Middlesex Hospital. She told him that her mother wasn't very well, and that she had to look after her younger brothers.

"You take as long as you like," he assured her. "Families always come first." And of course he made her feel guilty for lying.

The day was unusually dark, and every room in the hospital had its lights on, and it was beginning to rain.

Kelly waited for over an hour, reading old *Woman's Own* magazines and staring out of the window at the ambulances coming and going. Then she was ushered through to meet Dr Dipak Patel.

He wore hugely-magnifying spectacles and a blue striped shirt and he smelled of Extra-Strong Mints. He examined the hairs on the back of her wrist, tugging at them, peering at them, trying to extract one or two of them with his tweezers. In the end he said, "This is very unusual. These hairs are all different colours and textures, as if they belong to different people."

"My doctor said you could use electricity to get rid of them."

"I don't know. I can't tell you anything until I have made some trichological tests. Usually, everybody has one hair type. Brown, black, red, you know. And as they grow older, they turn all different kinds of white and grey. But what you have here, Miss O'Sullivan – well, it's quite remarkable. You have hairs of different colours, but you also have hairs of different thicknesses and different textures. Look at this, under the microscope. This is one strand of your own hair, here. Take a look. It doesn't match any of the others. Each hair is different, as if we had plucked them at random from different people waiting at a bus-stop."

"So what's happening to me?" asked Kelly. "They keep growing and growing, and twining themselves together."

Dr Patel raised both hands in surrender. "I'm sorry, Miss O'Sullivan, I really don't know. This is my first experience of anything like this. I have to wait for preliminary tests, you know, otherwise I might make a misdiagnosis."

"I see," said Kelly, feeling more alone than ever.

Dr Patel took hold of both of her hands. "I will give you all the help that I can. What else can I tell you?"

She went back to Sissuz feeling even more stressed-out than she had before. Even Kevin's impersonation of Mrs Bartlett couldn't make her smile. And all the time she couldn't stop herself looking at the basement door, and the upside-down *ankh* that was painted on top of it.

When Simon came back to the salon after lunch, he was in a seriously bad temper.

"That woman upstairs, she's driving me *mad*!" he shouted.

"Oh, come on, Simon," said Kevin. "Surely you can come to some kind of arrangement?"

"Arrangement? I've offered her everything! I've offered her money. I've offered to find her an alternative flat. I've even offered to pay all of her moving costs. But will she budge? Oh no! 'This is my flat and this is where I'm going to stay, me and all of my smelly cats!' I think she gets a perverse pleasure out of it. I think she enjoys watching me beg."

"Perhaps we ought to find some new premises," Kevin suggested. "If you can't expand here, why don't you look for a building where you can?"

"Because I'm not letting some stubborn old bag stand in my way, that's why! I'm trying to develop an exciting business here. It's just what this area needs. And we'll all make money out of it – not just me. I'm not going to have my whole career brought to a standstill by some doddering old biddy with a flatful of stinking cats!"

He had to calm down because his two o'clock lady came in – Mrs Fellows, the wife of the chairman of the local rotary club. But behind his easy patter and ingratiating smile, Kelly could see that he was still simmering with anger. He snapped his fingers at her to take Mrs Fellows to the backwash, and he barked at Susan because she was standing in his way. Kevin rolled up his eyes in a silent appeal to the heavens above.

By the time he had finished with Mrs Fellows, however, Simon seemed to have cheered up. He was gossiping and laughing, and he tugged off Mrs Fellows' robe like a bullfighter, and swung it around. "There!" he said. "A star is born!"

"Ooh, you're a flatterer," Mrs Fellows chided him, patting her curls.

Simon said, "Kelly, tidy up my station, would you? And take all those sweepings down to the basement."

Kelly swept up all of Mrs Fellows' grey, curly hair and tipped it into a black rubbish bag along with all of yesterday's hair. She had been trying to avoid going down to the basement, but Simon was watching her now and there was nothing else she could do. She switched on the light and cautiously went down the stairs, stopping and listening at every step.

There was another bag of hair down there, resting on top of stack of cartons. She kept her eye on it as she crossed the basement floor, but it didn't stir.

As she walked back to the stairs, however, she thought she heard somebody whisper, right behind her – so close that she could feel chilly breath on the back of her neck. She froze, one hand on the banister. She listened and listened, not daring to turn around, but all she could hear was the music coming from the salon upstairs, and Kevin laughing at his latest joke.

She thought: *no, I'm imagining it. I've probably been imagining all of it*. But as she started to climb the stairs she was sure that she heard the whisper again.

"*Beëlzebub … l'un des plus grands malheurs … il estoit froid comme la glace…*"

The voice was thick and laboured, as if the speaker's throat were half-choked with chilly phlegm. There was some more muttering, which Kelly couldn't make out, and then something about "*le diable … il est réel.*"

She didn't turn around but she was sure that she could hear the bag of hair shifting, centimetre by centimetre. She had a crawling feeling between her shoulder blades that went all the way down her back, and her mouth was dry with fear. She took one step upward, and then another, but the further she climbed up the stairs the more stairs there seemed to be, until the half-open salon door looked as if it were shrinking away from her.

"*Beelzebub … aussi vilain est abominable est au sorcier d'y aller de son pied que d'y entre transporté de son consentement par le diable…*"

More whisperings, more mutterings. Now there seemed to be a chorus of them, on every side. She was sure that she could feel fingers, plucking at her sleeves. She was sure that something was very close behind her – something terrible and huge – but she didn't dare to turn around to see what it was.

She tried to climb the stairs faster, but stairs seemed to pile upon stairs, as if she were trying to climb the wrong way up a moving escalator. The salon door shrank further and further away, and the light in the basement began to flicker and dim. If she didn't get out of here now, she would be swallowed up in darkness; alone and defenceless against whatever it was that was living in here.

"*Beelzebub…*" whispered the voice, and then burst out into uncontrollable laughter.

Kelly burst into tears. She stopped climbing because she simply couldn't climb any further. She stood on the staircase with her eyes tight shut and all she could do was pant in fright.

"*What's the matter, Kelly*?" said an echoing voice, a million miles away.

Kelly kept her eyes tight shut and gripped the banister even harder.

"*What's the matter, Kelly*?" the voice repeated.

Slowly, Kelly opened her eyes. She looked up and Simon was standing at the top of the stairs, looking down at her. "What's the matter?" he repeated. "I wondered where you'd got to. And, hey, you look like you've been crying."

"I'm all right," she said, trying to wipe her eyes with her fingers. "I haven't been sleeping very well, that's all."

"You should try hot chocolate, last thing at night, with three sugars. I swear by it."

Kelly closed the basement door behind her. She thought: *why don't you tell him? Why don't you say what you and Ned saw down here last night? You know that he'll understand.*

Yet she remembered what Ned's grandfather had advised him, and said nothing.

After supper, she phoned Ned, but his mother said that he was out. She wanted to tell him what she had heard in the basement, that name *Beelzebub*. She had heard it before, she was sure of it, but the O'Sullivans didn't have an encyclopaedia at home, so she hadn't been able to look it up. Perhaps Ned could find it on the Internet.

She was about to put the phone down and go and watch television, when the shopping list with Miss

Paleforth's number on it dropped out of her address book. She hesitated for a moment, but then she punched it out, and waited while the telephone rang and rang and nobody seemed to want to answer it.

She was a second away from hanging up when she heard Miss Paleforth say, "Yes? Kelly? Is that you?"

"How did you know?"

"I always know who's ringing me, before I ever pick up the phone. Every ring has a different sound, you know. A different sense of urgency. Yours was urgent, but you weren't at all sure if you ought to ring me up or not, were you? That's why I waited – to see how persistent you'd be."

Kelly took a deep breath. "What you said to me … about the devil-hair. Do you think I could come round and see you?"

Miss Paleforth said, "It's serious, isn't it? It's getting worse?"

Kelly said, "Yes," and it was all she could do to stop herself from crying again.

"Come round straight away, then. Don't stop to talk to anybody else, not even your father and mother or your very best friend. And God be with you. You'll need Him now, I promise you."

Miss Paleforth lived in a small semi-detached house at the very end of a long suburban cul-de-sac, backing on to the railway. From the outside, her house looked as if nobody had lived in it for years. The front gate was sagging on its hinges, the front garden was choked with yellowish weeds, and the maroon paint on the front door had faded almost to grey.

There were grubby net curtains hanging at the living-room windows, and the only signs of life were two bottles of fresh milk sitting on the doorstep, and a large cross-eyed tortoiseshell cat sitting beside them.

There was a bronze knocker on the front door with the face of a malevolent goblin. Kelly rapped three times and waited, and the cat mewed and rubbed itself around her ankles. “Here, puss,” she said, and reached down to stroke it. But as she did so, the cat hissed and glared at her and backed away, just like Mrs Marshall’s cat.

The door opened and there was Miss Paleforth, wearing a headscarf and a long red velvet dress, and a black beaded shawl.

“Come in,” she said, putting her arm around Kelly’s shoulders and ushering her into the hallway. As she did so, she looked up and down the street as if she were making sure that nobody was watching them.

The inside of Miss Paleforth’s house was gloomy and smelled of stale incense, but it was warm. There was clutter everywhere: an old-fashioned bicycle was propped up in the hallway, as well as an elephant’s-foot umbrella stand, dozens of pairs of boots and shoes, an accordion and an artist’s easel.

“You’ll have to excuse the mess,” said Miss Paleforth, picking up the hem of her dress so that she could high-step over a stack of old books. “I don’t know why I keep all this stuff, but it just seems to accumulate, you know, like flotsam washed up on the beach.”

She led the way into the kitchen, where an old-fashioned solid-fuel stove was burning. The kitchen was even more cluttered than the hallway. A pine dresser stood against the end wall, crowded with decorative plates and cups and storage jars, and draped with trailing plants.

In the centre stood a heavy pine table, with even more storage jars on it, as well as bundles of dried herbs and tangerine pomanders and wrinkled-looking roots.

"Do sit down," said Miss Paleforth, and dragged out a large pine chair. "I wonder if you'd like a cup of St John's Wort tea. It's very relaxing, helps you to clear your mind. And it's supposed to have other properties, too. In the middle ages they called it 'the devil's flight'."

"No, no tea, thanks," said Kelly. She looked around at all the jars of herbs and spices and she was beginning to wish that she hadn't come here.

Miss Paleforth sat down beside her and took hold of her hand. She looked very intently into her eyes. "You made the right decision," she said.

"What do you mean?"

"The decision to come here and see me. It was the best thing you could have done. You can go to all the doctors in the world, but none of them can help you. Not with electrolysis, not with surgery, not with radiotherapy. Your problem isn't caused by anything physical. It's caused by evil."

Kelly pulled back her sleeve and showed Miss Paleforth how much the hairs had grown, and how they were beginning to entangle themselves together. Miss Paleforth gently pulled at them, teasing them apart. "What did the doctor say?" she asked.

"He's sending me to Middlesex Hospital for tests."

"So he couldn't tell you what you're suffering from?"

"No. He said he'd never seen anything like it before."

"You're going to the hospital … why did you suddenly decide to come and see me?"

Kelly took a deep breath. "Something happened last night … down in the basement at the salon. My friend Ned and me, we went down there to see if anybody was squatting there."

"But there wasn't anybody squatting there?"

Kelly shook her head.

"There was something down there, though, wasn't there?"

"Yes," said Kelly. Her throat was so tight that she could hardly speak, but gradually she managed to tell Miss Paleforth all about the snakelike form that had come sliding after them up the stairs, and how they had managed to escape it.

Miss Paleforth listened carefully, and as she listened she kept on gently pulling at the hairs on Kelly's wrist. At last, when Kelly had finished, she said, "I used to be a doctor, you know, out in Martinique, in the Caribbean. That was years and years ago, when I was – well, when I was younger than I am now."

"You're not old," said Kelly.

Miss Paleforth gave her a wan smile. "Nice of you to say so, but I'm very much older than I look. When I was in Martinique I became interested in alternative medicines: herbs, and spices, and curative diets. I also became interested in the power of the mind to cure the body. It can do that, you know. But equally, the power of the mind can make the body sick. Good can cure, you know. But evil is a kind of infection.

She paused for a moment, still stroking, still tugging. "How long have you had these hairs?"

"Only two or three days. It's only ordinary hair swept up from the salon floor, but it just stuck on me, and started to grow."

"That's because somebody spoke the words over it. Somebody brought it to life. Somebody turned it from ordinary hair into devil-hair. Give me your hand."

Reluctantly, Kelly took hold of Miss Paleforth's hand.

"Now, squeeze my fingers as hard as you can."

Kelly immediately pulled her hand away. "I mustn't! I'll break your knuckles!"

"I thought so. Devil-hair gives you incredible strength. In Martinique, the story goes that people used to let it grow all over them, so that they would become almost superhuman, and take their revenge on people who had done them wrong. You could never get away from a man covered with devil-hair because he could walk straight up walls without a ladder."

"But how do you get rid of it?"

"The legends say that there are only two ways. One is to blow it off in a hurricane, which is rather difficult to do, here in Rayner's Lane. The other is to burn it off with fire."

"Burn it off? Surely electrolysis is just the same."

"You still don't understand, do you? Devil-hair isn't part of *you*. It's part of something else."

Kelly looked at Miss Paleforth for a long time. She was so eccentric, Kelly didn't know whether to believe her or not. But she could see something special in those pale, pale eyes of hers. A look of weariness, but a look of experience, and of genuine caring.

Miss Paleforth said, "I saw this done in Martinique, nine or ten years ago. I only saw it once, but the doctor who did it wanted me to watch, so that I would know exactly what to do, if it ever happened to me. Of course, when I came back to England, I never thought that I would ever see devil-hair again. But here you are, you've got it. And I'm probably the only person in the country who can get rid of it for you."

"You can really get rid of it?"

"Really. It'll hurt you a little but it won't burn you and it won't leave a scar."

"Can you do it now?"

"If you want me to. If you trust me."

"Yes," said Kelly, swallowing.

Miss Paleforth tugged the sleeve of her jumper up even further and laid her bare forearm on the table. "All right so far?" she asked, and Kelly nodded.

Miss Paleforth got up and went across to the dresser. She came back with half a bottle of light Jamaica rum. She poured a large measure into a glass and for a moment Kelly thought that she was going to drink it. But instead she produced a cigarette lighter, and flicked it into flame, and began to pass the flame from one side of the glass to the other. Up, down, across, loop. Watching her closely, Kelly gradually realized that she was forming the shape of an *ankh*.

Kelly flinched as Miss Paleforth passed the flame close to her face, but Miss Paleforth said, "We don't have to go on with this, if you don't want to. The choice is yours. The devil-hair won't spread all over you, I can promise you that, because it wasn't you who conjured it up. It wasn't you who wanted it. You probably caught it by accident.

"But you have to get rid of it one way or another. Otherwise it's going to stay with you for the rest of your life, like an illness that you can never shake off. It's going to make you feel tired and depressed and anti-social. You won't feel like seeing any of your friends any more. And as for love – nobody with devil-hair can ever fall in love. They're always trying to cope with the feeling that they don't belong to the world any more; that they've always got one foot in hell."

Miss Paleforth was right. Ever since the hair had started growing on her wrist, she *had* been feeling tired and out of sorts. And when Ned had asked to see her again, she had found herself half-hoping that he wouldn't bother, because she had too much on her mind.

"*Bet say lest*," whispered a hoarse, echoing voice in her ear.

She stared at Miss Paleforth with her eyes wide open.

"*Bet say lest, Beelzebub*," the voice repeated.

"Do it," said Kelly, so quietly that Miss Paleforth could hardly hear her.

"You're absolutely sure?"

"*Do it*!" Kelly screamed at her, and was electrified by the sound of her own voice.

Miss Paleforth swirled the rum in the glass and said, "*Skin and nails and hair and rings. Back to the place of all dead things.*" She swirled it faster and faster, reciting the words over and over, and then she dipped the flame of her cigarette lighter into the rum and lit it.

It burned for a moment with a spitting blue flame. Then – without any hesitation – Miss Paleforth poured it over the hair on Kelly's wrist, still flaming, and said, "*Turn tail, devil, and be gone*!"

Kelly let out a piercing shriek. Her whole wrist was engulfed in fire. She could see the hairs shrivelling, but the pain was intense, and she wrenched her hand free from Miss Paleforth's grasp and waved it wildly from side to side. The flames made a flaring noise with every wave, and leapt even higher. She was almost hysterical but Miss Paleforth was completely calm. After a little while she stood up, went over to the sink, and held a tea towel under the tap.

She came over to Kelly and wrapped the damp tea towel around her wrist and tightly held on to her hand. "You're all right, Kelly," she kept repeating, and her voice became quieter and more reassuring every time she said it. "You're all right. You've done it. You've got rid of the hair."

Kelly wept. "I never knew anything could hurt so much."

"I know. But it wasn't *you* that was hurting. It was the piece of the devil that you were banishing from your body. It doesn't hurt now, does it? And look."

Miss Paleforth unwrapped the tea towel. Kelly's forearm was smudged with red, but apart from that it was unblemished. No blisters, no burns, no scars whatsoever. And what was more, the hairs were gone, all of them.

"I can't believe it," she said, running her right hand up and down the back of her wrist.

"I told you. Fire, or hurricane. That's the only way you can get rid of the devil-hair."

"But, look, I'm not even *scorched*, and I had flames coming right out of my arm. How could I not be burned?"

"The people in Martinique say that fire is like a wilful dog. If you let it have its way, it will tear up everything in sight. That's why you have to be strict with fire, so that it will only burn what you want it to burn. And that's why you have to be strict with evil, too, or else it will infect everything around it."

Kelly said, "I don't know what to say. Thank you. I'll buy you some flowers."

"Well, that's a very kind thought. But I'd like more than flowers, if you don't mind. I'd like to see this basement of yours."

"*You* want to see it?"

Miss Paleforth nodded. "Whatever's hiding down there, Kelly, it needs to be dragged out into the light, and dealt with. I've seen this kind of thing before, in the Caribbean; and I've seen what happens when it's left unchecked. You're afraid of death? We're all afraid of death. But this is worse than simply dying, believe me."

She filled the kettle and put it on the hob. Then she said, "I sensed that there was something wrong at Sissuz, the very first time I went in there to have my hair done. I couldn't think what it was, but it reminded me so strongly of the feeling that I'd experienced in Martinique, I had to keep coming back, until I found out what it was. Didn't you ever think it was strange that a messy person like me could have her hair done so often?"

"We'll probably have to wait until Simon's day off," said Kelly.

"The sooner the better," said Miss Paleforth. "Now, how about some of that St John's Wort tea?"

When Kelly got home that evening, she phoned Ned again. He had just driven back from Basildon, and he sounded very tired.

"Ned, I've got rid of the hair!"

"What? How did you do that?"

"Miss Paleforth did it for me. She burned it off."

"*Burned* it off?"

"Yes, and it's totally gone. She was a doctor once, out in Martinique, and she seems to know an awful lot about all this mystical stuff. She's going to come and see the basement for herself."

"Do you think that's a good idea?"

"Well, why not? She might be able to get rid of it, whatever it is."

"But she's a bit of an oddball, isn't she? How are

we going to get people to believe us if we've got somebody like *her* helping us? They'll think we're as nutty as she is."

"She's not nutty. She's really sensitive. She really understands."

"Well, let's talk about it tomorrow. I'll try to meet you at lunchtime, OK?"

"OK … and by the way, I think I might have something that will help you look on the Internet. The last time I opened the cellar, I heard the name *Beelzebub*."

"That's a name for the devil, isn't it?"

"I think so. But you could try looking it up, couldn't you?"

"All right … if I get the time."

Kelly hung up. She knew that Ned was tired, but she was disappointed that he hadn't been more enthusiastic. She went into the kitchen, where her mother was cleaning the top of the stove, and put her arms around her, and gave her a hug.

"What was that for?" smiled her mother. "You don't want to borrow any money, do you?"

Kelly shook her head. "That was just because."

When she arrived at work the next morning, Mrs Marshall's black cat Isabel was sitting outside the back door, mewling. Kelly picked her up and stroked her and this time Isabel didn't make any attempt to scramble out of her arms.

"What's the matter, Isabel?" Kelly asked her. "Won't your mummy let you in? That's not fair, is it, on a cold day like this!"

She unlocked the back door and went across to the control panel to switch off the burglar alarm. If the alarm was still on, poor Isabel must have been outside for most of the night. Without even taking her coat off, Kelly carried her up the stairs that led to Mrs Marshall's flat. Her fur felt freezing, and she kept letting out these piteous little sneezes.

Kelly could smell the cats even before she reached Mrs Marshall's door. She could hear them, too, all yowling and crying. Isabel turned her head and mewed something at her.

She rang the doorbell. There was no reply, so she rang it again. After a while she knocked on the frosted glass panels of the door and called out, "Mrs Marshall! Mrs Marshall! It's Kelly from the salon! Are you all right?"

Still no reply. Perhaps Mrs Marshall was still asleep. After all, she had once told Kelly "I do love my bed, 'specially in the cold weather." But she was usually up and around by nine o'clock, even if she was still in her dressing-gown. Sometimes she came shuffling downstairs to borrow a spoonful of instant coffee or a tea bag.

"Mrs Marshall?" Kelly rang and knocked simultaneously, but there was still no response. She dropped Isabel on to the landing and went back downstairs. There was a spare key to Mrs Marshall's flat in the tiny side-room that Simon rather grandly called his "office".

She found it, and climbed back upstairs, where Isabel was still waiting for her on the landing. Perhaps Mrs Marshall had suffered one of her "turns", as she called them; or more likely she had taken a sleeping pill and hadn't woken up yet. Simon's constant pressure on her to move out of her flat had made it very difficult for her to sleep.

Kelly unlocked the door and called out, "Hello? Hello? Is anybody there? It's Kelly, from downstairs."

Three cats came trotting towards her, crying and mewing and jumping up. They were obviously hungry and thirsty.

"Hello? Mrs Marshall?" Kelly stepped into the living-room. It was wallpapered with brown flowers and furnished with an old brown three-piece suite, a coffee-table with china ballerinas and clowns on it, and a high-seated armchair with Mrs Marshall's knitting tucked into one corner of it. She was knitting herself a winter hat, in brown.

"Mrs Marshall? It's Kelly. Is everything all right?"

She was followed by cats, cats and more cats as she went along the narrow corridor and looked into the kitchen. She felt like the Pied Piper. The kitchen was in chaos. Empty bowls of cat food were littered around the floor, and the sink was full of dirty plates.

The rubbish bin was overflowing with empty Kattomeat tins and crumpled-up boxes of ready-made meals for one. One cat was perched on the windowsill, licking the droplets from the dripping tap. Another was nibbling at a chicken bone that it had managed to pull out of the rubbish.

The smell was overwhelming: rotten food, sour milk and cats' pee. Kelly had to press her handkerchief over her nose.

She looked into the bathroom. This was empty, too, but it smelled even worse, because this was where Mrs Marshall kept all of her cat litter trays. Kelly thought that she would never be able to look at a cat again, after this.

She tried the bedroom door. It opened a little way, and then it stuck, as if something soft and heavy were lying against it. Perhaps the carpet had rucked up.

"Mrs Marshall?" Kelly called out. "Are you all right, Mrs Marshall?"

She tried pushing the door again, but she could open it only six or seven centimetres. There was a different smell in here: the pungent smell of Vicks Vapour Rub and something else. A *dark* kind of smell. A smell like the black place beyond the archway in the basement. A smell like all the things that had ever really disgusted her.

"Mrs Marshall?"

Kelly decided to give up. She was probably making a fool of herself, anyway. Mrs Marshall often went around the corner shop in the morning to buy herself bread and milk and a copy of the *Sun*. In fact, Kelly could hear footsteps coming up the stairs now. That would be her, coming back.

"Mrs Marshall!" she said, with relief, going back to the sitting-room. "I'm sorry I let myself in, but Isabel was locked out at the back, and—"

It wasn't Mrs Marshall. It was Kevin. He looked around the room and wrinkled up his nose in disgust. "Phew, what a pen-and-ink! What are you doing up here? You know I can't start the day without my cup of instant."

"I was looking for Mrs Marshall. I rang her doorbell but she didn't answer."

"Hmm," said Kevin, picking up a china horse and putting it down again. "She's probably gone round to the corner shop."

"That's what I thought … but it's funny that she hasn't fed her cats."

"Maybe she's run out of cat food. I should think this lot probably get through a couple of hundred tins a week. Have you taken a butcher's around?"

"Everywhere except the bedroom. I couldn't open the door."

"Well, I suppose we'd better make sure. What a smell! It's enough to make a maggot gag!"

He ambled along the corridor, calling out, "Mrs Marshall! Mrs Marsha-a-all! You've got visitors! Better put your dressing-gown on!"

He went to the bedroom door and pushed it. "You're right," he told Kelly. "There's definitely something lying against it."

He put his shoulder to it and gave it a push. It budged another three or four centimetres. He grunted and gave it another push, and then another. Gradually, puffing and blowing, he managed to push it halfway open.

The bedroom curtains were closed, and it was dark and stuffy. On the opposite side of the room there was a walnut wardrobe with an oval mirror in it, and they could see themselves peering into the gloom, their faces pale and anxious. They could see the end of Mrs Marshall's bed, with its beige candlewick bedspread, and they could see a fraying Lloyd Loom chair with a dressing-gown hanging over it.

"Mrs Marshall?" said Kevin, in a voice that was very much higher than he'd meant to. Then, deeper, "Are you in there, Mrs Marshall?"

He looked around the door. He stayed silent and perfectly still for a moment, as if he couldn't work out what he was looking at. Then he turned back to Kelly and his face was even paler than before. "I think it's Mrs Marshall," he said.

"You *think*?"

He took a step back, and held on to her arm. "Listen, I don't think you ought to go in there. The best thing we can do is call the Old Bill."

"What's happened? Is she dead?"

"You really don't want to know, Kelly, I promise you. Let's go downstairs and dial 999."

"Oh my God, what's happened to her?"

Kevin tried to speak but then he had to clamp his hand over his mouth to stop himself from being sick. "Fresh air," he mumbled, and hurried along the corridor and out of the front door, leaving Kelly outside the bedroom.

She didn't want to look but at the same time she felt a terrible, overwhelming curiosity. She hesitated, watching herself in the oval mirror in the wardrobe. She ought to look. She ought to see what had happened to Mrs Marshall. But what if it was so bad that it gave her nightmares for the rest of her life?

But it was then that Isabel, the black cat, came padding along the corridor. She sniffed, and looked up at Kelly as if she were asking what she was supposed to do now.

"Don't go in there," Kelly told her. "You don't want to see your mistress dead."

Isabel started a harsh, rattling purr. Then before Kelly could stop her, she walked into the bedroom and jumped up on to the end of the bed.

"Isabel, come here!" Kelly called her. "Come on, puss, you can't stay in there!"

But Isabel remained where she was, sitting upright, her ears flattened, her head slightly arched back.

"Isabel, come here, will you?"

Kelly thought that she could reach into the bedroom and grab her without having to look at Mrs Marshall. Do it quickly, and keep your eyes on the cat. Then out again.

"Isabel, come on, puss. Be a good girl."

She took two quick steps into the bedroom and seized Isabel around the middle. She wasn't going to look at Mrs Marshall. She was going to keep her eyes averted. She was going to walk straight out of the bedroom and along the corridor and out.

But then she looked.

10

Detective Inspector Brough came down from Mrs Marshall's flat and stood outside in the yard for a minute or two, breathing deeply. It was so cold that it looked as if he were smoking. He was a short, stocky man with a sandy little moustache, bright blue eyes and surprisingly delicate hands, as if he would be good at needlework.

"Would you like a cup of tea?" Kelly asked him.

"That would be welcome."

A young detective sergeant came down the stairs, too. "Forensics want to know if you're finished up there, sir?"

"In other words, have I stopped poking about and getting in their way? Yes, Bryan, tell them I've finished. Oh – and get on to the RSPCA. We need somebody to take care of all these moggies."

"Yes, sir."

All of the cats were in a state of mewling confusion, except for Isabel, who stayed close to Kelly, winding herself around her legs and following her wherever she went.

Kelly handed DI Brough his cup of tea. He cupped his hands around it and blew on it, as if it were soup. "Did you see the remains?" he asked Kelly.

Kelly crossed herself. "Yes, I did. I wish I hadn't."

"I wish you hadn't, too. It's hard to believe that one person is capable of doing something like that to another, isn't it? It shakes your faith in human nature – and you're too young to start getting cynical.

He was silent for a moment, still blowing on his tea. Then he said, "Do you know anybody who could commit an act like that?"

Kelly shook her head. She kept seeing Mrs Marshall grinning at her. *Grinning at her*.

"Did Mrs Marshall have any enemies? Anybody who didn't like her? Or were there any kids in the neighbourhood who got a kick out of baiting her? Kids like that, they break in sometimes, and things get out of hand."

"I can't think of anyone."

"This boss of yours, Simon Crane. He didn't like her very much, did he?"

"Well, no. He wants to open a lifestyle centre upstairs, but Mrs Marshall refused to move."

"A lifestyle centre? What's that?"

"Oh, you know. A gym, with tanning beds, and step machines, and holistic massage, that kind of thing."

"I see. Doesn't sound like my kind of lifestyle. More of a pub man, me."

"Simon called Mrs Marshall an obstructive old cow. He was always arguing with her. But he wouldn't have *killed* her. He *couldn't*."

"Oh, yes? And why's that?"

"He's not that type of person."

"Nobody ever is. Just last week, one of the nicest lads I've ever met broke into an old lady's flat not half a kilometre from here, and hit her over the head with a brick. She was eighty-one. Died the next day in hospital. The boy got away with two quid and a toaster."

The detective sergeant came downstairs again. "We've double-checked, sir. There was no forced entry, but the bathroom window was off the latch."

"So the perpetrator could have got into her flat in one of three ways. A, he was somebody she knew, and she voluntarily let him in. Or B, he had a key and let himself in. Or C, he came in through the bathroom window."

"Mrs Marshall never let anybody in after we'd closed the salon," said Kelly. "That would have meant her coming all the way down the stairs, switching off the alarm, and opening up the back door."

"So, what if he had a key?"

"He would have needed a key to the outside door and another key for *her* door, and he would have had to know the alarm code."

"In other words, the only people who could have gained access to Mrs Marshall's flat after closing time were Simon Crane, and Kevin, and Susan, and you? Or anybody else that any one of you decided to let in?"

Kelly thought of Ned coming into the salon last night, but she thought it would be better if she didn't mention it. DI Brough would only start asking questions about what he had been doing there. And they had left together, so the murderer couldn't have been *him*.

"There's still the bathroom window," put in the detective sergeant. "And we found some stray hairs caught on the latch."

"What's the external access to the bathroom window?" asked DI Brough.

"I'm not sure. I came out to have a look for myself."

They all went out into the centre of the yard and looked up. "That's the window, there," said the detective sergeant, as they saw a police photographer's camera flash.

The window was ten metres up a sheer brick wall, with no nearby drainpipes or handholds of any kind.

"Well, either we're dealing with Spiderman, or somebody who goes around murdering people with a twenty-five metre extension ladder. I think we'll concentrate on A and B for now, particularly B. I want to have a chat with this Simon Crane fellow. What time does he usually get in?"

"Just after ten," said Kelly. "Do you want another cup of tea?"

"No, thanks, I'm awash." He stood beside her in the kitchenette while she rinsed out his mug. "Listen," he said, "what you saw today is going to take a lot of dealing with. I'm going to send somebody round to see you later, somebody who can help you to come to terms with it. And if you want to talk to me personally, here's my card."

Kelly took it, and said, "thank you". But then she said fiercely, "How can anybody *do* that? How can anybody tear another human being to pieces?"

DI Brough gave her a long, sad look. "I don't know, love. And I'm not sure that I ever want to."

Sissuz was closed all day, with all appointments cancelled. Police kept coming and going, as well as TV and newspaper reporters, and the man from the RSPCA to collect the cats, and a woman from the council's health department.

Simon came in at ten-fifteen, a few minutes before his first lady was due in. He looked tired and flushed, as if he had spent ten minutes too long under a sunbed.

"What's going on?" he wanted to know. "What are all these police doing here?"

DI Brough was talking to Susan, but he turned around. "Mr Crane? Mr Simon Crane?"

"That's me. What's going on?"

"Haven't heard the news this morning, sir?"

"I overslept. I had a shower and came straight to work."

"In that case, I'm afraid I've got some rather distressing news for you, sir. Mrs Marshall was found dead in her flat this morning. Murdered."

Simon stared at him. "Mrs Marshall? I don't believe it! Who would want to kill Mrs Marshall?"

"That's what I'm here to find out, Mr Crane."

"Well, I'll help you in any way I possibly can. I can't say that I liked her, but that's not the point, is it?"

"You had something of a dispute about a – lifestyle centre, wasn't it?"

"That's right. I needed the flat upstairs to expand my business, and she – well, she didn't want to move, that's all. I suppose you can understand how she felt: she'd lived there for donkeys' years. But it was a hell of a nuisance, I'll admit. It was costing me a fortune in solicitor's fees."

"At least you're open about it," said DI Brough.

"I can afford to be open. I didn't kill her. I was at home all night, at Harrow-on-the-Hill. My sister and her husband were staying with me."

"That's finc for now," said DI Brough. "But perhaps you could come down to the station later, and we'll talk in a bit more detail, if we can."

"Whatever I can do."

DI Brough put his arm around Kelly's shoulders. "You might also give this young girl a couple of days off, if she feels she needs it. And Kevin, too. They both found Mrs Marshall's remains and I can assure you that it wasn't a very pleasant sight."

"Oh, Kelly," said Simon. "I'm so, so sorry. How are you feeling? You can go home now, if you want to."

"I don't know … perhaps I'll stay for a little while longer."

"It's entirely up to you. But I could run you home, if you like."

At that moment the phone rang and Susan answered it. "Kelly, it's for you. Ned."

Ned said, "Are you all right? I've just heard about the murder on the news. They mentioned your name."

"I think I'm a bit shocked, that's all. It doesn't seem real. Simon's going to drive me home in a minute."

"Is there anybody there? At home, I mean?"

"Well, no, there isn't. Not during the day. But I can go to bed and rest."

"Let me come and pick you up. At least you'll have someone to talk to. And I need to talk to you, too. I've been doing some research into Beelzebub. There's all kinds of information on the net. Some of it's nothing but myths and legends and folk stories.

But there's a whole lot that's true, and it's really scary."

"What about the devil-hair? Did you find out anything about that?"

"Loads. I'll tell you about it when I see you."

"All right, that'll be great."

She hung up. "That was my boyfriend," she told Simon. "He's going to pick me up instead."

"Ah well," said Simon, with a regretful smile. "So long as you're in safe hands, that's all that matters."

Ned took her to the Willow Tea Room, in Pinner. They sat in a quiet corner next to the fireplace and Ned ordered a pot of tea for two, and a plateful of cakes. "You need something sweet after an experience like that."

"Ned, it was so horrible, I don't even want to think about it."

"Are you sure you're OK? You don't want to go and lie down or anything?"

"I'm fine. I'm really glad you called."

He poured her some tea, and she stirred three teaspoonfuls of sugar into it. He produced a large brown envelope, and took out pages and pages of scribbled notes.

"I looked up *Beelzebub* on the Internet, and this is only part of what I found."

"Really? All this?"

Ned fanned it all out. "I wouldn't have believed

any of this, if I hadn't seen that snake for myself. This is all supposed to be myth, and legend, and superstition. But when you've seen it with your own eyes, you realize that most of it is fact, or based on fact. There's a whole world out there which we refuse to believe in, because it doesn't seem to make any logical sense. But what's logical about anything?

"Beelzebub is the prince of demons, second only to Satan. His name means 'lord of the flies', but recent research by Jesuits has shown that this probably refers to the fact that his statue was always dripping with sacrificial blood, and so it attracted a great many flies."

"Ugh," said Kelly.

"I know," said Ned. "But this is important. According to an ancient book called *In Zodiaco Vitae*, Beelzebub was tall, and incredibly strong, with piercing eyes. He was also covered from head to foot in thick hair."

"Devil-hair," said Kelly. "Just like Miss Paleforth said."

Ned nodded. "According to what I found on the Internet, the Jesuits believe that Beelzebub is always trying to find a foothold in the real world. He thinks that if he can find favour with men and women, God will have to admit him back into heaven, which is where he *really* wants to rule. They say that demons and angels actually exist. Not with horns and claws. Not with feathery wings and haloes. But they exist.

They're supposed to be the very essence of good and evil, and they're always at war, and they always will be, right up until the Day of Judgement."

"So what about the hair?" asked Kelly.

"Ah … this took quite a lot of digging, but I found it in the end. The story of the devil-hair goes back to the seventeenth century, in the Caribbean. In those days, when sailors cut their hair, they used to stuff it into flour-bags, to make themselves comfortable pillows. Full of lice, probably, but comfortable."

"Ugh," Kelly, repeated.

"You can't judge these guys. Everybody was filthy in those days. They thought you were being too fussy if you had a bath once a month."

"Anyway … and this is the real coup: there's a website on sorcery in the Caribbean in the seventeenth century. In 1643, a party of French sailors landed on Martinique, and went inland, looking for whatever they could find. By chance they met up with a small colony of exiles called Les Grand Sorciers de Dieu, the Great Magicians of God. These people had been banished in 1630 from Aix-en-Provence in France because they were suspected of raising up demons and devils. They were supposed to have invited demons and devils to possess them, so that they could have powers like flying, and turning blood into wine, and walking on water."

"And did they?" asked Kelly.

"Did they what?"

"Did they fly, and walk on water?"

"There's no proof that they ever did. But they were supposed to have learned their sorcery from magicians in Egypt and North Africa. They believed that they were doing God's work because all demons and devils have to obey God's holy command; and because they thought that God had given Moses demonic powers to turn his staff into a snake, and to bring the seven plagues to Egypt, and to free the children of Israel.

Ned leafed through his notes. "Les Grands Sorciers were tried in France and sentenced to death for witchcraft. But the strange thing was that nobody could execute them. Every man who tried to put a rope around their necks started to choke and suffocate and cough up blood. So in the end the magistrates sent them off to Martinique, in a galleon marked with the sign of the *ansate* cross, in lamb's blood."

"The *ansate* cross?"

"The cross with a loop at the top. Just like the *ankh*. It was the only way they could ward off ancient Egyptian magic."

"So what happened when the French sailors found them?" asked Kelly.

"The sailors brought them something which they had in very short supply, and that was human hair. They needed hair if they were going to raise up

Beelzebub. Hair, and lots of it. They slit open the sailors' pillows, and then they cut an upside-down *ankh* on their chests, so that thirteen drops of blood fell into the hair. After that they had to recite the incantation. It said on the website that the original incantation is under lock and key in the British Library. But the first words of it are '*Bête céleste*,' meaning, the beast from heaven."

"*Bet say lest*," Kelly whispered. "That's what it was. The first words to raise up the devil."

Ned said, "Yes. That's what it was. And you just happened to be down in the basement when it was happening. Because while the incantation was being spoken, the magicians would plunge their arms into the hair, and it would quickly grow all over them, in the same way that it grew on you. They ended up looking like the demon Beelzebub himself, covered in thick hair from head to foot. In fact, in a way, they *were* the demon Beelzebub. They had all of his powers, so that they could climb into people's houses at night, and take whatever they wanted, or murder people they didn't like. They could walk straight up vertical walls, and across ceilings too, like spiders. And they could hide almost anywhere. You could open your eyes at night and see one of them crouching in the corner of your ceiling, in the shadows, watching you.

"Between them, the French sailors and Les Grands Sorciers formed an unholy alliance. The magicians turned the sailors into hairy men so that they could go out and raid the local ports and villages. In return, the sailors brought them food and wine and supplies. The sailors even smuggled several of the magicians back to Europe.

"In the end, though, everything went sour. The sailors grew tired of relying on the magicians to turn them into hairy men. They wanted the incantation for themselves. Of course, the magicians refused to tell them what it was. That incantation was the only bargaining point they had, to make the sailors bring them supplies. There were fights and arguments. In the end, the magicians were supposed to have cast a spell which set fire to all of the sailor's ships, and sent them to the bottom of the harbour, along with all of their plunder. In return, the sailors burned down the magicians' colony, and killed all the magicians, and as far as anybody knows, that was the end of them all.

"You can look it all up. It's on www.beelzebub.com."

"But that happened hundreds of years ago," said Kelly. "You don't really think that the same thing's happening here?"

Ned gave her an emphatic nod. "It all fits, doesn't it? The hair. The same words, all in French. The name Beelzebub. And now two people murdered by somebody who managed to enter their flats by climbing up totally vertical walls."

"And?" said Kelly.

"And isn't it obvious? What was the only thing those two murdered people had in common – apart from the way that they died? Richard Walker was a society hairdresser and Mrs Marshall was an elderly cat lady. But they both had some connection to Simon Crane."

Kelly said, "It can't be Simon. It just can't be."

"I don't have any proof that it is, I'll admit it. But think about it, Kelly. Who else could it be? We searched that basement ourselves and there's nobody else down there, is there? Whispering voices, yes; and hair that can turn itself into a snake, yes. But no tramps, no squatters. Only this hair – and this evil power that can turn it into something much more than hair."

Kelly rubbed the back of her wrist. "That's what Miss Paleforth told me. That I'd been touched by something totally evil."

"And it made you feel bad, didn't it? It made your hand strong, but it made you feel bad. Imagine what it must feel like, if you let the hair grow all over you? Imagine how strong you must be. But imagine what terrible thoughts must be going on inside your head. Anger, vengeance, hatred."

"I still can't believe it's Simon. He's been so nice to me."

"I don't know. Perhaps it isn't him. But he could be like Dr Jekyll and Mr Hyde, couldn't he? When he's normal, he's the nicest guy you could ever hope to meet. But when he's covered up in that devil's hair … he's frightening. He's like a mad beast who doesn't know the difference between right and wrong."

Kelly said, "What if it isn't him?"

"It doesn't matter. It could be Kevin. It could be Susan. It could be somebody we've never met. But whoever it is, we can't let them kill anybody else, can we?"

"So what do we do?"

"I don't know, but I'm thinking about it."

"I think I should ask Miss Paleforth. Perhaps she can help us. If she took the hair off my hand … perhaps she can find a way of getting rid of it altogether."

"Why don't you ask her?" said Ned.

Kelly nodded. She was beginning to feel weak and shaky, and Ned took hold of her hand. "It's all right," he said. "You're suffering from delayed shock. Don't let's talk about this any more. I'll take you home, and we can talk again tomorrow."

He paid for their tea, and walked her across to his car, with his arm around her waist. She wasn't a dependent person, but she was beginning to feel that she needed him. As he drove her home, though, she found herself hoping that he was wrong, and that Simon had nothing to do with either of the two murders.

* * *

On the eleven o'clock news that night, it was announced that after four hours of questioning about the killing of Mrs Violet Marshall, hair stylist Simon Crane had been released by Harrow Police. His solicitor said that his alibi was "unassailable".

"He was in bed in his third-floor flat in Harrow-on-the-Hill when the tragic attack on Mrs Marshall took place. This has been confirmed not only by his sister and his brother-in-law, who were staying overnight on the sofa-bed in his living-room, and were still awake at the time in question, unable to sleep; but also by CCTV videotape taken from security cameras in the entrance hall to his block of flats, which showed nobody leaving or re-entering the building between 1:11 a.m. and 6:27 a.m.

"Similarly, Mr Crane has been cleared of all suspicion of the recent murder of the West End hair stylist Richard Walker. Again, witness and CCTV evidence show beyond a shadow of a doubt that Mr Crane did not and could not have left his flat that night."

His solicitor paused for effect, and then he added, "Not unless he flew."

Kelly was sitting on the couch, wrapped in a blanket. The gas fire was on, which was something of a luxury in the O'Sullivan household, and her mother had brought her a mug of hot chocolate. All the same, she felt that she would never be warm again, ever.

"Are you all right, my pet?" her mother asked her. Out in the hallway there was a deafening clatter and a cry of pain. Patrick was trying to bobsleigh down the stairs on a tin tea-tray, just because he'd seen people doing it in comics.

"Patrick!" shouted her mother. "If you're going to kill yourself, will you do it quietly?"

Kelly reached out and took hold of her hand. This was a moment when she needed her mother more than ever; but she also knew that it was no use her asking her mother to face up to her demons for her. That was something she would have to do for herself.

"I'm all right, Mum. I promise."

"Don't be having nightmares, that's all."

But of course she did.

In her nightmare she was freezing cold. She was wearing nothing but a thin white cotton nightdress. The bedroom was dark, except for a dim blue flickering light. She had to strain her eyes to see.

The bed was right in front of her, still draped in its candlewick bedspread, although the room was so gloomy that it was impossible to tell what colour it was. She didn't want to approach the bed, but she was irresistibly drawn towards it. She kept her eyes tightly closed because she didn't want to look. *She didn't want to look.*

Her knees touched the end of the bed. Through

her nightdress, the mattress felt damp and cold. There was a smell which she couldn't describe. The smell that darkness would have, if darkness ever had a smell. The smell of rivers at night. The smell of places where you weren't supposed to go.

She didn't want to open her eyes. She didn't want to look. She clenched her fists so tightly that she dug her fingernails into the palms of her hands. But she knew that if she didn't look, she would have to stay here, hour after hour, until she *did* look.

"*Help me*," she whispered. But her voice didn't even echo; and nobody replied.

She didn't know how long she stood there, with her eyes tight shut. But the bedroom was growing colder and colder and she was beginning to shiver. She heard noises, too. Scratching noises, that could have been rats. Ring-tailed rats, or something far worse.

She took a deep breath of icy air.

And opened her eyes.

And it was exactly what she had seen in Mrs Marshall's bedroom, except that it was lit by this flickering blue light, and everything was so much colder, and everything was so much clearer.

Mrs Marshall's severed head was nailed to the wall, high above the bed. Her eyes were open and her mouth was open and her tongue was hanging out. Her grey hair was wildly awry, almost as if she had been electrocuted.

Both of Mrs Marshall's severed hands were nailed to the headboard, one on each side. And both of Mrs Marshall's severed feet were lying at the bottom of the bed, one on each side.

Kelly slowly swivelled her head away, and as she did so she saw what had been preventing her from pushing open the door. Mrs Marshall's headless, empty body.

I want to wake up, she said, in a slow, blurry voice. But the nightmare continued. She heard scratchy-sounding footsteps in the corridor outside Mrs Marshall's bedroom, and the cats started to yowl in a horrific chorus that made the hairs prickle on the back of her neck.

Something's coming. She panicked. *Is this a dream or not? If it's not a dream I have to start running. It's after me, it's going to tear off my head and nail it on to the wall, next to Mrs Marshall's. It's going to cut off my hands and feet.*

Run, she heard herself saying, in a weak, strangled voice. *Run*.

She was still gargling the word "run" when she woke herself up. She was shivering and her nightgown was clinging to her. Siobhan's luminous alarm clock told her that it was 3:32 a.m. Siobhan herself was staying with friends tonight, so Kelly was alone.

I won't run, she said, as she straightened her pillow. Not just won't, but *can't*.

11

The next morning, Simon was full of good humour. He smiled at everyone, and he was especially attentive to Kelly.

"How are you feeling?" he asked her. "You can always take some more time off if you need it."

"No, I'm fine. I'd rather keep busy. Otherwise I start thinking about Mrs Marshall."

"I just hope they catch whoever did it. It's frightening to think that there's somebody around who could kill a defenceless old lady like that.

Kevin raised an eyebrow, but Simon saw him and immediately said, "I didn't like Mrs Marshall, I admit it. I've never made any secret of it. I told the police that I didn't like her. But just because I didn't like her – just because I wanted her out of that flat –

that doesn't mean that I'm pleased about her being killed like that. It could have been you who was killed like that. It could have been Kelly. It could have been any one of us."

At that moment, Isabel stalked into the salon and started to sniff around.

"What's that cat doing in here?" Simon wanted to know. "That's one of *hers*, isn't it? I thought they'd all gone to the RSPCA."

"I asked if I could keep her," said Kelly. "She won't be a nuisance, I promise. I'll make sure that she doesn't get in the way and I'll take her home this evening."

"I can't have a cat in the salon."

"Why not?" asked Susan. "The customers will love it."

"I just can't, that's all. Health and safety regulations. We serve sandwiches and coffee. Supposing we get cat hair in them?"

"In *here*, you're worried about one or two hairs?"

"I'm sorry, Kelly. I'm not having a cat in here, and that's final."

He approached Isabel and held out his hand. "Here kitty, kitty. Let's go for a little walk, shall we? Out to the back yard, which is where you're going to stay."

Isabel arched her back. Her tail stiffened into a rigid brush and the fur on her spine stood up. Simon came closer and she started to spit and hiss at him.

"I don't think that cat likes you an awful lot, Simon," said Mrs Hyde, in Kevin's chair.

"It's half-wild, that's the trouble," said Simon. "That woman never cared for those cats properly. She never made sure that they were house-trained, and they were always rummaging in the dustbins out at the back."

"No, no," Mrs Hyde insisted. "It doesn't like you, that's all. I've got cats of my own. I know when they take exception."

"Come here, you stupid cat!" Simon snapped at Isabel, and made a grab for her. Isabel lashed out with her left paw and scratched the back of his hand.

"Ouch!" said Simon, sucking his wound. "Did you see what it did?"

"Only defending herself, Simon," Kevin remarked.

Furious, Simon made another grab. This time Isabel lashed out at both of his hands in a flurry of sharpened claws. Then she jumped up on to the back of Mrs Hyde's chair and made a startling leap at Simon's face.

"*Gaahhhhhh*!" Simon shouted, as Isabel landed on his shoulder and ripped at his cheek. He spun around, trying to wrench the cat off him, but she caught her claws in his hair.

"*Get it off me! Get it off me!*"

Kelly said, "Hold still, for goodness' sake, you're frightening her even more!"

"*Get it off me, I said!*"

Simon was slapping and pulling at Isabel's fur, but now she was standing on top of his head, her claws digging into his scalp. Kelly managed to dodge around behind Simon until she could reach Isabel's tail. She pulled it hard, but Isabel only yowled and hung on. Kelly pulled her tail again, and this time Isabel came scrabbling off the top of Simon's head – his long blond curls still entangled in her claws.

They all stared at Simon's hair, lying on the salon floor. They all stared at Simon, who was almost completely bald, his scalp criss-crossed with scarlet clawmarks.

Kelly eased Isabel's claws out of Simon's wig, and then picked it up and handed it to him. "I'm sorry," she told him. There was nothing else that she could say.

Simon took several deep breaths. Without his mane of shining blond hair, he looked very much older; and his lean good looks had something of the vulture about them, something fleshless.

He made no attempt to put his wig back on again. Instead, in a quivering voice, he said, "Everybody get back to work. I'm going off to Birmingham now, and I won't be back until tomorrow. Kelly – get rid of that cat. I don't care how you do it, but get rid of it. If I ever see it anywhere near this salon again, I'll send for the vet and have it put down."

"Yes, Simon. I'm sorry, Simon."

Simon took his wig and walked out of the salon.

He slammed the back door so hard that a mug fell off the draining-board. They heard the tyres of his BMW squealing and then he was gone.

"Oh God," said Kelly. "I didn't mean to embarrass him like that. I feel awful."

"I never guessed he was bald," said Susan. "Never in a million years. It makes him look quite creepy, doesn't it?"

"One of the best syrups that I've ever seen," put in Kevin, admiringly.

"Syrups?"

"Rhyming slang, dear. Syrup of figs, wigs."

Kelly sat down on one of the chairs. Without warning, her eyes filled up with tears, and she began to sob. Susan put her arm around her and shushed her. "Come on, you've had a terrible shock. Why don't you let it all out?"

Halfway through the afternoon, Miss Paleforth came into the salon. She was wearing a long green coat and a woolly hat and she was carrying a Sainsbury's bag crammed with crochet and celery and cushion-covers, as if she had been around town collecting things that began with "c".

Kelly was sitting at the reception desk. Miss Paleforth leaned over her and said, in a very quiet voice, "I heard on the news about what happened upstairs. Terrible. I dropped in to see if you were all right."

"I'm OK, thanks," said Kelly. "But I had a terrible nightmare about it last night."

"The police said it was some kind of ritual murder."

"It was horrible. I don't even want to think about it."

Miss Paleforth watched her sympathetically for a while, saying nothing, but then she said, "I need to know just one thing."

Kelly looked up. Miss Paleforth's eyes were strangely unfocussed, as if she were staring *into* her, rather than *at* her.

"I need to know about the head, and the hands, and the feet. The police didn't give any details, you see. They just said 'ritual murder' and that was all."

Kelly hesitated. After all, DI Brough had specifically asked her not to discuss what she had seen in Mrs Marshall's bedroom with anyone.

But Miss Paleforth said, "Were they … detached?

Kelly nodded; and Miss Paleforth nodded, too.

"That's what I was worried about. I was hoping that it was just a coincidence, this murder happening here. But the head, and the hands, and the feet. That settles it. In Martinique, if anybody is ever killed like that, then you know that the devil-hair has been involved. That's because you can't go to heaven without your head to sing praises to God, and your hands to put together to pray, and your feet to walk through the fields of the Lord."

She lifted her eyes and furtively looked around. "I

need to go down to the basement," she said. "I need to see this thing for myself."

"Can't we just leave it?" said Kelly. "Can't we just forget about it? I've been thinking of leaving Sissuz and looking for a job somewhere else."

"Just help me get down to the basement," said Miss Paleforth. "That's all I ask. Just help me to get down there once, and then, yes, it would probably be better if you left here for good, and went as far away as possible."

"Why do you have to go down there? Why is it so important?"

Miss Paleforth was silent for a long time. Then she said, "There was a doctor once. A very good doctor and a very good man. I met him in Martinique. If he'd lived ... well, if he'd lived, I wouldn't have stayed 'Miss' for the rest of my life. But he challenged a mystic healer, and the mystic healer took a terrible revenge on him. A ritual revenge.

"That's why I need to go down to the basement. Because I swore to myself that if ever I came across the works of Beelzebub again, I would hunt him down and I would root him out. My doctor couldn't go to heaven, but I am going to do whatever I can to make sure that Beelzebub goes back to hell."

"You know about Beelzebub?" whispered Kelly.

"My dear, I have dedicated my life to knowing about him. I know him so well that I can *smell* him."

"All right. Come back here at twenty to seven. Everybody else will have gone by then."

"Thank you," said Miss Paleforth. "If we do this now, we may save many, many lives. Not to mention souls."

After Miss Paleforth had left, Kelly called Ned on his mobile phone. "I'm stuck in a traffic jam in Ealing," he told her. "I hope it's not urgent."

She told him about Miss Paleforth. "Can you come round to the salon tonight? I don't want to go back down there without you."

"I don't want you to do *anything* without me."

"Pardon?"

"You heard. I like you too much. In fact I think I might actually love you."

Kelly could feel the heat in her cheeks. "You can't love me. You hardly know me."

"That's no excuse. Haven't you ever heard of love at first sight?"

"I don't know," said Kelly. She was amazed at how pleased she was. When she put down the phone, she sat at the reception desk with her hand over her mouth, trying not to smile.

Kelly felt hungry at six o'clock, so she bought herself a chow mein flavoured Pot Noodle. She could only eat a few spoonfuls of it, though. The kitchen at the back of the salon still smelled vaguely of cats and when Kelly smelled cats she thought of Mrs Marshall's head, grinning at her, her eyes bulging, nailed to the wall.

She scraped the rest of the Pot Noodle into the bin.

Isabel wouldn't be parted from her. Wherever she went, Isabel kept tangling herself between her legs, and when she sat down in Susan's chair, Isabel hopped up on to the shelf next to her and wouldn't take her yellow eyes off her, purring in a deep, rattling purr.

"We're going to find out what happened to your mistress, Isabel. I promise you."

Isabel didn't answer, of course, but her rattling purr grew louder and louder, until it sounded almost like a nestful of rattlesnakes, or one of those whirling rattles that the Mexicans use to celebrate the Day of the Dead.

Kelly leaned forward and looked into Isabel's eyes but Isabel didn't flinch. She felt sure that Mrs Marshall's spirit was inside her somewhere, a human looking out through a cat's eyes, unable to speak, unable to tell anybody who had murdered her, but determined to get her revenge.

"I have to perform a bit of a ritual here," said Miss Paleforth. "Some of it will sound like hocus-pocus, but it's what they do in Martinique, and if it works in Martinique, there's no reason why it shouldn't work here. Maybe most of it's nonsense, but I was talking to a priest about exorcisms once, and he said that he didn't like to leave anything out, no matter how silly it sounded, in case he left out the bit that really did the trick."

"You're going to perform an *exorcism*?" asked Kelly.

"Oh, no. Not like *The Exorcist*. More of a chasing-away. If there are any evil spirits in the basement, we'll soon get rid of them."

"I'm frightened," Kelly admitted. But Ned put his arms around her shoulders and said, "Come on, I'm here. Everything's going to be all right."

Miss Paleforth reached into her bag and produced a small hessian sack, tightly tied with twine. She opened it up, and poured a little of its contents into the palm of her hand. "Salt," she explained. "Nothing like it for protecting you against evil spirits. In medieval times, nobody would walk around the house at night without a handful of salt, just in case they met the devil."

She tossed salt all around the salon. "This will prevent any spirit from staying here, once we've chased them out of the basement. And it will stop them from coming back, too. Evil spirits are worse than nesting birds. They always like to come back to the same dark corners."

She approached the basement door. She took out a thick red crayon, and drew a cross over the upside-down *ankh*. "That will get rid of any bad luck," she said. "Now, let's go down and see what we can see."

She opened the basement door and Kelly quickly switched on the light for her.

"You're quite right to be frightened," she said. "Anybody who says they aren't frightened of evil is a fool. But we always have to face up to our fears, sooner or later, or else they will come back to haunt us another day."

"All the same, I think I'll stay up here," said Kelly.

"Please, Kelly. I need all the help I can get. I need people who *believe*. You can't imagine how many evil spirits escape punishment or chasing-away because people simply refuse to believe in them."

Kelly hesitated. She really didn't want to go down into the basement again.

Miss Paleforth took hold of her hands. "Kelly ... it was you who brought me here. You asked for my help because you knew how terrible this thing could be. Now I need *your* help. Otherwise, I'm just a single voice, crying out against a whole cacophony of evil spirits."

Ned said, "Come on, Kelly. I'll be right beside you all of the time."

Kelly looked up at him and nodded. "All right. But if anything really horrible happens—"

"If anything really horrible happens we'll all be out of there like rockets," Miss Paleforth assured her. She produced a large torch, switched it on, and said, “Come on, then. It’s now or never.”

12

Miss Paleforth led the way down the stairs and Kelly and Ned followed at a safe distance. The basement was very quiet this evening. Even the constant dripping seemed to have stopped. Occasionally they felt the subterranean rumble of a tube train pulling out of Rayner's Lane, and the strange chorus of sighs that followed it, as draughts blew through the ventilation shafts and crevices in the cellars. It was like a ghostly choir – a choir which had never existed, yet which sang every five or ten minutes, all day and into the night.

The bags of hair and rubbish were heaped up against the right-hand wall. Beyond them was the alcove – so dark that even Miss Paleforth's torch couldn't penetrate it.

Miss Paleforth set out five small candles on the floor, in a pentacle pattern, and lit them. They smelled strongly of evergreens, and something that reminded Kelly of mothballs.

"Come close now," she said. "What we're going to do tonight is purify this place, so that nothing evil can stay here, and no evil deeds can be performed here again. Evil is a kind of infection, and what we're going to do is disinfect this basement, in the same way that you'd disinfect a sick-room. You understand me?"

"Yes," said Kelly; and it was only then that she realized that her teeth were chattering.

"Ned," said Miss Paleforth. "I want you to bring me that bag of hair, and lay it down on the floor in the middle of these candles."

Ned went across and hefted up the bag. "Feels revolting," he said. "All *crunchy*."

He laid it down in the middle of the pentacle. Miss Paleforth shook more salt over it, and said, "Spirit of darkness, you cannot hide any longer. Spirit of evil, you cannot crouch in this darkness any more. We are here to bring you out into the light. We are here to dismiss you."

For a moment it looked as if nothing was going to happen, but then the salt began to crackle and spit and sparkle bright blue, as if it had been tossed on to a gas ring. Tiny oval holes appeared in the plastic bag, and the hair inside began to protrude – stiff and curly and speckled with dandruff.

"I command you to return to the place where you came from," Miss Paleforth cried out. "I command you to return and never to visit this place again. I command you never again to exploit the weakness of those who would use your powers for their own selfish ends. And I declare this place clean, and pure, without a single blemish. A place where evil spirits will never dare to hide again."

There was a long, long silence. Then Miss Paleforth said, "I think we could pray now, don't you?"

All three of them closed their eyes and prayed in silence for a while. The ghostly choir of draughts sang all around them. Kelly prayed for Mrs Marshall's soul; and for Richard Walker, too, although she had never known him. But she prayed most of all that Beelzebub would leave this basement and vanish out of her life for ever.

Miss Paleforth eventually cleared her throat. Kelly and Ned opened their eyes and looked around. "Well..." said Miss Paleforth. "I think we've done it. The place certainly *smells* fresher."

"Then it's over?" asked Kelly. "No more whispering, no more snakes, no more murders?"

"Let's hope so."

"Thank you," said Kelly. "Really, thank you. And I'm sorry I was so scared."

Ned said, "That's it, then? That wasn't difficult at all, was it? I mean – as long as you know the right things to say."

Miss Paleforth bent down to blow out her candles. As she did so, however, Kelly heard a rustling sound, and the bag of hair in the middle of the pentacle began to move – almost as if something was inside it, trying to force its way out.

Miss Paleforth slowly stood up, and backed away.

"What's happening?" asked Kelly; but Miss Paleforth could only say, "*Sssh!*"

The bag of hair suddenly burst wide open, making them all jump. A great bulge of hair came out of it, blonde and brunette, russet and grey. Gradually, right in front of their eyes, this bulge of hair began to take on a recognizable shape – a huge head, thick-necked, with heavy overhanging brows and a hooked nose. It could have been a real head, except that it was made out of nothing but human hair, rippling and flowing with every movement it made.

Kelly clung on to Ned's arm, and watched with rising terror as the head slowly turned around so that it was facing them, and opened blind eyes that were made of nothing but hair. There was a long pause, and then it spoke, with lips that were made out of hair, too.

"*So, you think to dismiss me, do you, you weaklings?*"

"Who are you?" Miss Paleforth demanded, although her voice was very shaky. "Tell me if you're the one that I'm looking for."

The head gave a thin, aggressive growl. "*I am the prince of evil, my darling. The lord of the flies.*"

"Beelzebub?" whispered Miss Paleforth.

"*Only my shape, not my substance. This hair – what is it? It is nothing but human detritus. It is the spirit inside that gives it a face, and a voice, and a mission. You wanted to see me, my darling, and here I am.*"

"I dismiss you," said Miss Paleforth, and threw a handful of salt right into its face. The salt crackled, and the hair sizzled and scorched, but the head did nothing but laugh – that same, lewd laugh that Kelly had heard in the cellar before.

"I dismiss you back to the depths of hell where you came from," said Miss Paleforth. Her voice was almost hysterical. "I dismiss you, I dismiss you, I dismiss you!"

"*I didn't come from hell,*" Beelzebub replied. "*Not originally. I was once a child of heaven. One day – with the help of man and womankind – I shall return there, to my rightful throne, and sit among the angels once again.*"

Kelly was clutching Ned's arm so tight that he had to pry her fingers loose. "It's not true, is it?" she said. "Ned, tell me this is a nightmare. Tell me I'm asleep."

"If it's a nightmare," said Ned, "then I'm having it, too."

"*I dismiss you, you foul spirit!*" Miss Paleforth screamed at Beelzebub. "This place is clean now, and free from your infection! You must go, and never come back!"

"*You have no power to dismiss me, my darling*," said Beelzebub. "*I am only here because I am believed in.*" His hairy lips stretched back in a terrible grin to reveal his hairy teeth – and then a long hair tongue licked out. "*How about a kiss, my darling? Don't they say that love conquers all?*"

Miss Paleforth threw the rest of her salt at the hairy head, but again Beelzebub did nothing but laugh at her. Then the head began to rise from the heap of hair, higher and higher, on a neck that was thick and long as a python. It began to nod and sway towards them, its eyes wide, its mouth still grinning.

Miss Paleforth stood in front of it, mesmerized, her face completely drained of colour.

"*Let's go!*" shouted Ned, grabbing hold of her arm. "Come on, Kelly, you too – let's get out of here!"

Miss Paleforth stared at him as if she couldn't understand what he meant.

"*Let's go!*" Ned repeated. More and more of Beezlebub's neck was pouring out of the bag of hair, and the head was almost touching the ceiling.

They scrambled up the stairs as fast as they could. Halfway up, Miss Paleforth stumbled and dropped her bag. Combs, make-up, hairslides, beads and loose change scattered all over the stairs.

Gasping with hysteria, Miss Paleforth tried to pick everything up; but Ned said, "*Leave it!*" and almost lifted her up to the top of the stairs. Beelzebub's head was already rising up towards them, his mouth crammed with ever-increasing rows of razor-sharp teeth.

They reached the top of the stairs, hurried into the salon and slammed the door behind them.

They stood looking at each other, breathing hard.

"Now what do we do?" asked Kelly.

Miss Paleforth sat down on one of the salon chairs. "I don't know ... I really don't know. Plainly I don't have enough influence to be able to chase him away. Did you hear what he said? *I am only here because I am believed in*. Whoever conjured him up in the first place believes in him, so strongly that he or she has given it life. We have to find out who that person is, and stop them."

"Well, I'm sure that it's Simon Crane," said Ned. "He might have had an alibi which satisfied the police, but he was the only person who knew both Richard Walker and Mrs Marshall. And if he turned himself into one of these hairy men he could have climbed out of his flat without anybody seeing him, and into both Richard Walker's flat and Mrs Marshall's flat, straight up the wall."

"What do you think, Kelly?" Miss Paleforth asked her.

Kelly said, "I didn't want to believe it, but I think Ned's right. There's nobody else here who could have conjured up that spirit. Susan wouldn't have done it, or Kevin."

"You're right," Miss Paleforth agreed. "If it *is* Simon Crane, he's made a bargain with Beelzebub which only he can break – so nobody else can dismiss Beelzebub except him."

"How can we persuade him to do that?"

"I doubt if we can. Simon must have a very good reason for conjuring up a spirit as dangerous as Beelzebub, and if he refuses to dismiss him, there's nothing we can do. Well, except kill him."

"Supposing Simon was locked up?" said Kelly.

"That would work. If he couldn't get access to the hair any more, he wouldn't be able to turn himself into a hairy man. The hair is essential to the demonic possession."

"You're not thinking of kidnapping him, are you?" asked Ned. "Where could we keep him locked up? There's only my uncle's toolshed."

"Of course I'm not thinking of kidnapping him. I'm thinking of proving that he murdered Richard Walker and Mrs Marshall. Then the police would lock him up."

"If the police haven't been able to prove it, how can we?"

"We only have to prove that he committed *one* of them, don't we?" said Kelly. "You remember what they said about the Richard Walker murder? He was being blackmailed, but his desk was torn open and all of his papers and his accounts books had been taken. The murderer was probably the blackmailer, and he killed Richard Walker because he didn't want Richard Walker to tell the police who he was."

"And if the blackmailer was Simon Crane—" said Ned.

"Which is highly likely. He was working at Richard Walker's salon at the time Chrissy Black's hair was cut off. And there's a good chance that he might have kept those papers and those accounts, and hidden them somewhere."

"*Here*, do you think? In the salon?"

"I don't know," said Kelly. "But it's worth having a look."

They searched Simon's office, opening up every drawer and pulling them right out, in case he had taped the incriminating papers to the underside. They rummaged through the towel cupboard and the stockroom, and even looked inside the biscuit-tin and underneath the till.

"Well, I don't think they're here," said Ned, after half an hour of searching. "If he's still got them, he's probably hidden them at home."

Miss Paleforth suggested, "If they're really incriminating, he would have burned them, wouldn't he?"

"He might," said Kelly. "But Simon's very businesslike … very neat and systematic. He likes to keep a record of everything."

"So what if he *has* kept them?" asked Ned.

"He's away in Birmingham tonight, remember.

We can break into his flat and steal them. Then we'll have all the evidence we need."

"Are you out of your mind? Break into the flat of a man who can turn himself into a hairy demon and tear people into pieces with his bare hands?"

"What else can we do?" said Kelly.

"We could walk out of here and never come back, and forget that this ever happened."

"But it *did* happen, Ned! People died! And they're going to go on dying, as long as that thing stays down in that basement!"

"Kelly," said Ned, putting both hands on her shoulders. "You don't have to save the world. That's not your responsibility."

But Miss Paleforth said, "I disagree, Ned. Everybody is responsible for saving the world – whether it's from pollution or global warming or nuclear accidents or pesticides. Or evil. We're *all* responsible for saving the world."

Ned said, "We shouldn't do anything rash, Kelly."

"I'm sorry, Ned. We have to."

Ned lifted both hands in surrender. "Yes," he said. "I suppose we do."

Ned drove Miss Paleforth home. They agreed to meet up again at eleven-thirty that night. Ned had to drive his Uncle Sean to Heathrow airport to catch the Aer Lingus flight to Dublin, and Kelly had to take Isabel home, change and have her supper.

Kelly climbed out of the car to let Miss Paleforth out. Before she opened her garden gate, Miss Paleforth unexpectedly took Kelly in her arms and hugged her. "You're very brave," she said. "I shan't forget you, ever."

13

Ned took Kelly back to Waverley Road. She carried Isabel on her lap. Before he let her out of the car, Ned leaned across and kissed her on the cheek, and then the lips.

"You scare me, you know," he told her.

"Scare you? Why should I scare you?"

"We could forget about this Beelzebub thing altogether, couldn't we? It isn't really any of our business. But now you want to go breaking into Simon Crane's flat."

"You thought he was the murderer long before I did."

"I know. But thinking something is different from proving it."

"Ned … you should have seen what he did to Mrs

Marshall. We can't just let him get away with it. What are we going to feel like if he does it again, and again?"

Ned said, "You're right, of course. I'll be back at quarter past eleven." He kissed her again, and said, "You're a very special person, you know. I love you."

Kelly kissed him back and smiled, but she didn't say anything.

"Now, what's this?" said her mother, when she stepped into the hallway carrying Isabel under her arm. "Not another mouth to feed?"

"She's all right, mum. She doesn't have anywhere else to go."

Kelly let Isabel jump down on to the carpet and Isabel stalked up to her mother, sniffing at her.

"I think she can smell the supper on me!"

"Oh, no mum. She likes you. She can smell the difference between good and evil."

"In that case, she's very welcome! How about a saucer of milk for you, kitty?"

After supper, when all the dishes had been washed up, Kelly went upstairs and changed, while the rest of the family sprawled out in front of the television. Eleven-fifteen came and went. Eleven-twenty. Still no Ned. At eleven-twenty-five, Kelly went into the hallway and called Ned on his mobile.

His voice sounded crackly and faint. "*—stuck—*" he said.

"What's the matter?" she asked him.

"*—car's broken down – right by Heathrow – it's going to take hours—*"

"Well, call me as soon as you can. We have to break into Simon's flat tonight. We don't know when he'll be going away again. It's our only chance."

"*—call you back – I—*"

Kelly put down the phone.

"Is everything all right?" asked her mother.

"Fine, mum. Honestly." She picked up the phone again and dialled Miss Paleforth's number. The phone rang and rang but Miss Paleforth didn't answer. In the end she hung up, and sat frowning at herself in the hallway mirror. She couldn't believe that Miss Paleforth would let her down. Perhaps their experience with Beelzebub had frightened her off.

She had a choice now: either she could wait until tomorrow before she tried to break into Simon's flat and find his letters to Richard Walker, or else she could go by herself, and she really didn't like the idea of going by herself.

She called Kevin. "Kelly!" he said. "How are things with you? I was just wondering whether to watch the late-night news or fall asleep. In fact, I think I *was* asleep."

"How about doing something more exciting instead?"

Quickly – and trying not to sound too emotional – Kelly told him what had happened in the basement.

Kevin said, "You're not pulling my leg, are you? A *head*, made out of hair?"

"We all saw it, Kevin. We saw it and we heard it. It was so frightening I can't describe it. But we have to get rid of it. Simon's going to kill more and more people if we don't. Anybody who stands in his way."

"But breaking into his flat…"

"What else can we do? Oh, yes. We could look the other way and pretend it never happened. But what kind of people would we be if we allowed ourselves to do that? This is something from hell, Kevin, and it's arrived in our lives; and we have to find the confidence to send it back."

Kevin was silent for a moment. Then he said, "All right. You're right. I'll come and pick you up in twenty minutes. What do you think I ought to wear?"

"Black. We're burglars, remember?"

They met outside Dalmeny Court a little after midnight. The rain had eased off, although the evening was still wet and chilly. Kevin was wearing a black chenille sweater and Adidas tracksuit bottoms, and he was carrying a Tesco bag with a large screwdriver and a torch in it.

"I feel just like Raffles, the gentleman burglar," he said.

Kelly was wearing a black nylon jacket, a short black skirt, and thick black tights. "I feel like I'm going to a Halloween disco."

They crossed the busy road and walked across the semi-circular driveway. Then they went up the steps and into the brightly-lit lobby. There was a desk there, where the night security guard must have been sitting, because there was a half-empty styrofoam cup of coffee on it, and an ashtray with a dwindling cigarette, as well as a copy of *The Racing Post*. A closed-circuit TV camera screen showed Kelly and Kevin approaching the desk, and then peering around.

"They'll have us recorded on video," said Kevin, anxiously. "We won't stand a chance."

"If we find what we're looking for, it won't matter, will it? They won't charge us for breaking and entering if we've managed to solve two horrible murders."

"Well, I suppose you're right. I'm not used to breaking the law, that's all. I'm feeling quite short of breath."

"You brought your inhaler?"

"Oh, yes," said Kevin, and patted his top jacket pocket.

They waited for a moment, but no guard appeared, so they cautiously crossed the lobby and pressed the button for the lift. It seemed to take hours before the lift arrived, and as it did, Kelly heard footsteps on the opposite side of the marble lobby.

"Hey, wait a minute!" called a voice. It was the night security guard, with a pot belly and flappy trousers and very squeaky shoes.

He hurried up to the lift doors and held them open, so that they shuddered.

"It's all right," said Kelly. "We're friends of Mr Crane."

"Mr Crane is out tonight. He won't be back until tomorrow morning."

"He said we could crash here tonight if we needed to." Kelly held up a key – which was actually the key to the back door of the salon. Before the security guard could focus on it, she dropped it back in her pocket.

"Very well, then," said the security guard. "But I'll have to take your names for the visitors' book."

"Liam and Patsy Gallagher," Kelly replied, without any hesitation.

"Right, then. That's OK. I'll tell Mr Crane that you're here when he gets back, so that he doesn't disturb you."

"Very good of you," said Kevin.

The security guard hung around, as if he were expecting a tip.

"Very, *very* good of you," Kevin repeated, and pressed the button for the top floor.

"Do you think he suspected anything?" asked Kelly, as the lift took them up.

"Probably. You know what these security guards

are like; they've got nothing better to do than arrest impoverished old ladies for walking out of supermarkets with an individual shepherd's pie tucked under their cardigans. And yet the very next day – when that same shepherd's pie is beyond its sell-by date – they'll just chuck it away."

"You're not an eco-warrior, are you, Kevin?"

"Of course not. I just care about people, that's all. What do you think I'm doing here tonight?"

Kelly stood on tiptoe and kissed him. "There's more to you than meets the eye, isn't there?"

Kevin slapped his stomach. "By God I hope not."

They reached the orange-painted door of Simon's flat, number 1013. They looked and they listened, but they couldn't hear any music or talking, or even the sound of a television turned low.

"Right, he's definitely not in," said Kevin. "I'm going to try to force the door."

He took out his enormous screwdriver, and was just about to wedge it into the side of the doorjamb when there was a *ping*! The lift doors opened and a fiftyish woman in a black fur coat appeared, leading a skinny white poodle on a red-leather strap. She had a puffy, artificially suntanned face, like a half-collapsed soufflé.

"Hello," she said, as she passed them by. "I hope you're not going to make all that noise tonight, like you did last night. All that music. Bang, bang, bang.

And all that screaming. It sounded as if you were killing people."

"No, you won't get any of that," said Kevin, trying to sound light-hearted. "We're just going to spend a quiet night swapping postage stamps."

The woman gave him a swollen, disbelieving look, and dragged her diminutive dog down the corridor.

"The Lord alone knows what Simon gets up to," said Kelly. "Now, quick as you can, before anybody else arrives."

Kevin stuck the screwdriver into the side of the door and hammered it deeper with the flat of his hand. He eased it back, and there was a sharp splintering noise. Then, quite suddenly, the lock was sprung, and the door juddered open.

Kelly looked up and down the corridor to make sure that nobody had seen them. Then she pushed open the door and entered Simon's flat. Kevin closed the door behind them, and jiggled the lock so that it managed to stay shut.

Kelly switched on the lights. Simon's flat was large, but very bare, with plain white walls and plain black carpets on the floor. The furniture was minimal: a Swedish sofa, a low Japanese table, and black and white cushions scattered on the floor. There was an expensive Bang & Olufsen CD player too, and a tall black Japanese vase with a single artificial lily in it.

The bedroom was the same, with only a futon to

sleep on, and a large painting on the wall which consisted mostly of black, with a small crimson dot in the corner.

Through the bedroom, however, Kelly found a small office space, with a desk and a personal computer, and five black filing cabinets. These were all neatly marked with handwritten cards saying "Correspondence A–Z", "Invoices", "Sissuz Accounts" and so on. At the bottom right-hand corner there was a drawer marked "Miscellaneous".

"Let's try there first," said Kelly.

Kevin tugged the handle but the drawer was locked. "I'm sorry," he said, lifting his hands in defeat.

"You're sorry? What for? You opened the front door, didn't you? I'm sure you can open *that*!"

"I don't know … this is like burglary."

"Kevin, don't lose your nerve on me now. It's not *like* burglary. It *is* burglary. Now let's just get on with it, shall we, and make sure we do it well?"

Kevin thought about that for a moment, and then he said, "You're right. Better to be arrested for a five-course meal at the Savoy, rather than a bagful of fish and chips from down the road."

Kelly shook her head. "You're sounding more like my father every day."

Kevin forced his screwdriver into the drawer of the filing-cabinet and bent it back. Soon he had distorted the top of the drawer so much that he was able to knock away the lock. He scraped out the drawer and laid it on the desk.

"Here we are. Your 'Miscellaneous'."

There were all kinds of irrelevant bits and pieces in the "Miscellaneous" drawer. Press cuttings, brochures, bills from local restaurants, petrol coupons, advertising pamphlets from country house hotels. But underneath all of this, Kelly found a transparent plastic document case. She lifted it out in the way that detectives on television lift out evidence: between finger and thumb, barely touching it.

Inside the transparent case was a sheaf of paper, covered in neat columns of figures. But it wasn't the figures that attracted Kelly's attention so much. It was the bloody fingerprints, all over the paper. Dried now, but extremely clear.

"Bingo," she said, lifting out the first sheet of paper. "Look what it says here: *payments made to Simon Crane re Chrissy Black*. And look how much he was paying him! A lump sum of £25,000, and £4,500 every month."

"This must have been how he started up Sissuz," said Kevin. "Richard Walker was forced to finance him, and to pay his running costs. Sissuz was supposed to be a huge hairdressing franchise, with branches all over the country. But the trouble was, Simon never managed to keep his franchise-holders, and he always expected far too much. If somebody else opened up a Sissuz shop, he wanted eighty per cent of the takings. He had a good idea, but he ruined it because he was too greedy."

Kelly dropped the page back into its case. "*Now* we've got something to show the police. If these are Simon's fingerprints and this is Richard Walker's blood, we can prove that Simon committed both murders."

They replaced the filing-cabinet drawer as best they could, even though Kevin had bent it so much. They switched off the lights and walked back through the bedroom. But as they approached the living-room they heard the front door opening.

"Here!" whispered Kevin, and dragged Kelly into the shadows behind the bedroom door. They held their breath and waited and listened. There was no further sound for almost a minute.

"Must have been the wind," Kelly mouthed.

Kevin frowned and said, "*Ssh.*"

Another long silence passed, and then they heard something being knocked on to the living-room floor – a vase or an ornament, something like that. They heard a brushing sound, and then a deep grumbling noise.

"There's something out there," Kevin whispered.

"Whatever it is, we can rush it, can't we?"

"I don't know. Maybe it's just that security guard."

Without warning, all of the lights blinked off. The flat was plunged into complete darkness, except for a shaft of moonlight that fell through the bedroom doorway. Kelly and Kevin waited and waited. Kelly was sure that she could hear claws, scratching on the carpet. She was sure that she could smell something, too. A sickening stench, like rotten chicken marinating in water from long-dead chrysanthemums.

Something stumbled against the coffee-table. "Oh God, what is it?" whispered Kelly. "Oh God, I hope it's not—"

"It can't be," said Kevin. "He didn't even know we were coming here, did he? Come on – the best thing we can do is make a run for the door. We can be out of here and down the stairs before whoever-he-is can blink."

"All right," said Kelly, and gripped his hand tight. "On my mark – one – two – three—"

She hesitated for one long agonizing second, and then she said, "*Go*!"

They hurtled out of the bedroom door and across the living-room, hand-in-hand, but they were far too slow, and it was far too late. A huge dark shape came lunging towards them, and Kelly felt Kevin whipped away from her. "*Kelly*!" he screamed, but Kelly herself fell sideways, off-balance, and hit her back against the arm of the sofa.

"*Kelly! It's got me! Kelly*!"

She could hear Kevin's feet drumming against the wall, and she could vaguely see the shape that was holding him down. It was black and hairy and indistinct, and it smelled so foul that the bile rose up in the back of her throat.

She was terrified. Her every instinct was to run. But Kevin was kicking and screaming and she knew that she couldn't leave him.

"*Kelly! It's crushing me, Kelly! Kelly, do something for God's sake*!"

Kelly went for the light switch and jiggled it furiously up and down, but the lights still wouldn't come on. Kevin started to choke and wheeze. Kelly circled around the back of the sofa and tried to pull the hairy thing's arm. It felt thick and harsh and muscular and she was revolted even to touch it. But Kevin was wheezing even more desperately now, and so she dug her fingers into the hair and wrenched at it as hard as she could.

The hairy thing didn't even flinch. It swung its arm around and hit Kelly across the side of the head – a blow so violent that it made her ear sing. She fell backward against the wall and bruised her back against the low drinks cabinet in the corner.

"*Kelly – I can't – breathe—*" gasped Kevin.

Kelly tried to stand up, knocking over a bottle of vodka. Suddenly she thought of Miss Paleforth and her glassful of blazing rum. *Only two things can get rid of the devil-hair – fire and wind*. And here she had fire.

There was an ashtray on top of the drinks cabinet, too, with a book of matches in it. Kelly picked up the bottle of vodka, unscrewed it, and approached the huge stinking bulk of the hairy man, trying to keep out of his way. Kevin had stopped screaming now: all he could do was to fight for breath. As Kelly came nearer she heard a crackling sound and Kevin gasped in pain. The hairy man must have broken his ribs.

"I dismiss you! I dismiss you! I dismiss you!" Kelly shouted out, copying Miss Paleforth. At the same time, she emptied the vodka bottle all over the hairy man's head and shoulders, and splashed it down his back.

The hairy man let out a deep, angry growl, like several voices speaking at once. Kelly could hear Simon's voice but she could also hear voices that were barely human. She threw the empty vodka bottle aside, snatched up the matches and lit the whole book at once.

Orange light flared up; and in that first flare she saw how truly terrifying Beelzebub was. The head in the basement had been nothing but hair. But this creature had crimson eyes and a mouth cluttered with teeth as sharp as stalactites, and his long tongue thrashed from side to side like a silvery-black snake.

He raised one hand towards her, and she saw leathery fingers and hooked-over claws. This was every child's nightmare. This was the thing that *really* crouched under the bed. This was the thing that *really* hunched in the shadows on top of the wardrobe.

Kelly was so frightened that she almost forgot what she was supposed to be doing. She stood with the blazing matchbook in her hand and she couldn't move.

But then Kevin managed to choke out, "*Kelly – it's killing me*—" and she jerkily tossed the matches at it and stumbled two or three steps back.

Instantly, the hairy man burst into flames. He threw his head back and let out a terrible chorus of roars and screams, but the vodka blazed with a lurid blue light and engulfed him from head to foot in fire.

Kevin was screaming too. Kelly shouted out, "*Kevin! Get yourself free*!" She could see his legs kicking, but instead of releasing him, the hairy man was gripping him even more tightly.

Kelly jumped over the sofa and snatched Kevin's left hand. The flames poured out of the hairy man and orange sparks of burning hair flew up all around him. The heat was almost unbearable, and Kelly had to shield her face with her other hand. Kevin's screaming had become a high-pitched shriek. The hairy man had both blazing arms held tight around his chest in a defiant embrace. Kevin's chenille sweater was on fire and so was his hair. He struggled and thrashed as the flames scorched his face and hands, but the hairy man refused to release him.

The stench of burning hair was sickening and the whole room was filled with eye-watering smoke.

"*Save me*!" Kevin begged Kelly. "*Save me – I can't stand the pain*!"

But then the flat door suddenly opened, letting in a huge gust of air. It was the old woman from the flat next door. She cried out, "*Fire! Fire*!" but she had given the blaze just what it wanted. Refreshed with oxygen, the flames roared up to the ceiling, and the hairy man and Kevin became nothing but a funnel-like pillar of fire.

The old woman shielded her face with her hand, and slammed the door shut again, but by now it was too late.

There was no more screaming, no more furious bellowing. Only the soft, intense noise of a fire that was now so hot that it couldn't be extinguished.

Kelly kept back against the wall, watching the flames in helpless horror. She kept her hand over her nose and mouth, but all the same the smoke was suffocating.

It didn't take more than two or three minutes, however, before the flames began to die down. As they did so, Kelly could see that Kevin was dead: his face burned black, his scalp scarlet and raw, his clothes burned into smoking ashes. But in the very last flicker of flame, she saw that Simon was standing behind Kevin, still holding him upright, and that Simon appeared to be completely unscathed. His face and his shoulders were slightly reddened, but they weren't burned – just like Kelly's arm after Miss Paleforth had burned off the devil-hair.

The last flame died, and the room was swallowed

up in darkness. Kelly stayed where she was, breathless with fear. She heard Simon drop Kevin's body on to the floor. It fell with an awful crunch. Then she heard him walk through to the bedroom, and open up his closet and drawers.

She started to edge towards the door. She trod very carefully, because she didn't want to step on Kevin's smoking body in the dark. She had managed to negotiate her way around the sofa when the lights were abruptly switched on, and Simon appeared, dressed in a black roll-neck sweater and a pair of corduroy trousers. Without his wig he looked like a malevolent child.

"You see what you've done?" he said. "You've dared to defy one of the greatest powers on earth, and all you've managed to do is murder your own friend."

Kelly heard sirens, two or three streets away. She was trembling so much that she couldn't speak; and she didn't dare to look down at Kevin.

"I could have had plans for you," said Simon. "With Beelzebub's help, I could have built up a business empire, and you could have been part of it. Nobody could have stopped us. Nobody could have stood in our way. But you had to stick your nose in and ruin everything. What did it matter to you if Richard Walker died? You didn't even know him. What was so important about Mrs Marshall? The world's a better place without people like her."

The sirens were nearer now, and Kelly could hear people running along the corridor outside. "You're finished," she said, defiantly. "You're a cold-blooded murderer and you're finished."

"I shall never be finished, so long as I have Beelzebub on my side. But you will be, I'm warning you. I'm going to find you, Kelly O'Sullivan, one night when you least expect it, and for what you've done to me today I'm going to rip your heart out. That's a promise."

At that moment, the building supervisor and four or five men appeared, toting fire-extinguishers. "My God," said the supervisor, peering into the smoke. "What happened here?"

"Hell on earth," said Simon, and pushed his way past him. Kelly said, "Stop him!" but nobody understood what she meant.

"Stop him!" she repeated. "You can't let him get away!"

She struggled past two bewildered men and pushed her way into the corridor. It was crowded with firefighters now, and there was no sign of Simon anywhere.

A woman came up and put a pink blanket around Kelly's shoulders. "You're shivering, love. Why don't you come along to my place and have a nice cup of tea?"

14

DI Brough met her by the narrow brook that meandered through her local park. It was a bright, crisp morning, but it must have been squally out at sea because the park was crowded with seagulls. Three small boys were trying to pull a shopping trolley out of the brook without getting their trainers wet.

"How are you feeling?" DI Brough asked her. His sergeant was waiting by the car, eating a packet of Twiglets.

"Frightened," she said. "He's going to come and get me, I know he will."

"He hasn't turned up at the salon," said DI Brough. "We've tried four or five other addresses too. His mother's house. Some of his friends. Not that he's got many friends."

"I wanted to go and see Kevin's parents, to tell them how sorry I was, but I didn't even dare to do that."

"No, no. You're wise not to. I don't know how much of this Beelzebub story I believe, but he's obviously a very dangerous man."

"Did you check the fingerprints? And it was him that murdered Richard Walker?"

"Yes, and yes. We can't be one hundred per cent sure if that was Richard Walker's blood on those papers, but it was the same group, and we've sent it away for DNA sampling. Then we'll know for sure. We've been through Simon Crane's bank accounts, too, and it *was* him who was blackmailing Richard Walker. He took more than £345,000."

A mongrel dog ran across the park and sent the seagulls bursting up into the air, wheeling and screaming. DI Brough shaded his eyes with his hand and watched them. "Do you know what my grannie always used to say? That seagulls were the souls of sailors who had drowned at sea. That's why they always sound so sad. They can never come home again, you see."

"When do you think *I'll* be able to go home?" asked Kelly.

"Not before we catch this character. You'll be all right at your aunt's house, though, won't you, for a bit?"

"I suppose so. It's just that my whole world's been

turned upside down. Kevin's dead because of me, and I can't live at home any more, and I don't even have a job."

DI Brough nodded. "What we really need to do is flush him out."

"What do you mean by that?"

"Well, he wants his revenge on you, doesn't he? And it won't have escaped him that you're the only witness to what happened in his flat with Kevin. I know we've got plenty of circumstantial evidence, but it's certainly going to help our case if a jury can hear the full story right from the horse's mouth, so to speak."

He reached into his pocket. "Fancy a cough sweet?"

"No, thanks. What do you suggest we do, to flush him out?"

DI Brough popped a sweet into his mouth and rattled it around behind his teeth. "I don't know yet. It has to be something that will bring him out in the open. I don't want to risk anything happening to you, but at the same time I don't want him to have any chance of getting away. If we don't catch him first time, he'll be twice as wary the next time. And as long as he's out there, you're in very great danger indeed.

He gave his sweet a thoughtful suck, and then he said, "We'll just have to put our heads together, won't we?"

* * *

Ned came round to see her that evening. For the three days since Kevin's death, she had been living with her father's older sister Edie in her house in Roxbourne Road. Edie was a widow and very fussy and set in her ways. She actually had plaster ducks flying up the wall of her living-room and a toilet-roll cover in the shape of a crinoline lady.

Ned looked tired. He gave her a kiss and waved hello to Edie in the kitchen.

"The local council have been around to Sissuz, and taken all of the hair out of the basement. Simon Crane won't be going back there now. And neither will Beelzebub."

"He's going to try to find some hair from somewhere," said Kelly.

"Well, the police have advised all the local hairdressers to keep their eyes open. They can't do very much more than that."

They went into the living-room and sat down. Ned took hold of Kelly's hands and said, "That was a crazy thing you did, breaking into Simon's flat like that."

"I know. But I couldn't think of any other way of getting the evidence."

"You could have waited for me. I could have protected you."

Kelly shook her head. "You don't understand. You couldn't have protected me. Kevin tried to, and look what happened to him."

Ned said, "Perhaps I got hold of the wrong end of the stick. Perhaps you're not quite the girl that I thought you were."

"What does that mean?"

"I don't know. I suppose it kind of surprised me that you went ahead and burgled Simon's flat without me."

Kelly squeezed his hand. "This is the twenty-first century, Ned. You know, girl power and all of that."

"Yes, I suppose you're right. But I'm just an old-fashioned romantic."

Kelly leaned forward and kissed him. "There's no harm in that." All the same, she couldn't help thinking that he was acting strangely – almost like a different person.

That night, after Ned had left, Kelly went to bed in Aunt Edie's cramped little spare room. It still had Star Wars wallpaper and a duck mobile hanging from the ceiling. She pulled back the curtain a little way and looked out over the houses backing on to Aunt Edie's garden. She saw a couple washing up their supper dishes in a brightly-lit kitchen. She saw somebody in their bathroom, a pink blobby shape behind their frosted glass window. She saw televisions flickering behind tightly-closed curtains.

She felt very lonely, and excluded from all of this everyday family life. And she felt frightened, too. Somewhere, out in the night, a dark hairy creature was searching for her, a creature that could climb up walls and crawl across ceilings. It wanted her so badly that she could almost feel its hatred, as if the temperature had suddenly dropped, and something was scratching at her window.

She sat up in bed and flicked through two or three magazines that Siobhan had given her. They were full of the same old articles: how to attract boys, how to give yourself a makeover, how to dump boys, how to change your whole life in seven and a half minutes. Then she read last month's *Hair Stylist* magazine, although she wondered what the point of it was, now that she had lost her job.

Near the back of the magazine, however, she came across an article about the Creative Young Hair Stylist of the Year Award. A prize had been offered for the most talented young professional hair stylist – a helicopter trip for two people to Chattington Manor Country House Hotel in Warwickshire, a chance to design a new hairstyle for the next James Bond movie, and five hundred pounds worth of hair-styling equipment.

The closing date for the competition had already passed, and the prizewinner would be taking his or her helicopter flight on Saturday evening, in less than three days' time. But the winner's name wouldn't be publicly announced until Thursday evening, at a Gala Charity Dinner in London.

Kelly read the article twice, then she put it down.

What had DI Brough said? He wanted Simon Crane out in the open, where he couldn't get away. And what had Miss Paleforth said? The only way to get rid of the devil-hair is by fire, or hurricane.

She had tried fire, and the consequences had been dreadful. Perhaps it was time that she tried wind. She was determined that she wasn't going to let Simon Crane make her feel hunted and haunted for the rest of her life. She was determined to be free.

DI Brough said, "I'm going out on a limb for you. I hope you know that. If we arrange this little scenario and Simon Crane doesn't appear, I'll be lucky if I don't lose my pension."

"He'll come, inspector, I'm sure of it. He hates me so much."

"It's a very creative idea, Kelly, and none of my staff has thought of anything better. So, we're going to go with it. Provided your friend Susan agrees to it, that is."

"I've talked to her already. She's all for it."

"She knows what the risks are?"

Kelly turned to Susan and said, "Inspector Brough wants to make sure that you know what the risks are."

Susan came across and took the receiver away from her. "Detective Inspector Brough? This is Susan here. You listen to me. Kelly's my friend and Kevin was my friend and I will do anything to bring that Simon Crane to justice. *Anything*, do you hear me?"

"I hear you," said DI Brough. "I just hope you understand what you're up against."

It was front page news in the *Hair Stylist*, and it made page five in the *Evening Standard*, as well as all of the local papers. It was even mentioned on *London Tonight* on ITV.

"If Simon Crane doesn't see any of this," Inspector Brough remarked, "then he must either be dead, or hiding under someone's bed."

The grand winner of the Creative Young Hair Stylist of the Year Award was Susan Bright, from Sissuz in Rayner's Lane. She was commended for her Afro-Caribbean and Asian styles, and especially for a hairstyle she called "The Chop", which was a short angular haircut for young black girls.

Susan would be taking one other person on her prize helicopter flight to Chattington Park: her new junior stylist, Kelly O'Sullivan. Susan was reported to have said, "I want her to see what she can achieve, too, if she has the same determination, and the same vision, and the same will to succeed."

Kelly had said, "I'm too excited for words."

It was announced everywhere that the flight would leave at six o'clock on Saturday evening from Roxbourne Park.

* * *

She spent Saturday afternoon watching television. Isabel sat close beside her, and refused to let her out of her sight.

"What is it, kitty? You don't have bad feelings, do you? Well, believe me, you're not the only one."

Aunt Edie knocked on the door. Behind her – to Kelly's surprise – was her mother. She came up to Kelly and laid a hand on her arm and looked into her face as if she were trying to remember who she was; and to make sure that she would never forget.

"I had to come, darling," she said. "I wanted you to know that it's a very brave thing that you're doing."

"I don't have any choice."

"Of course you have a choice. Everybody has a choice, every day of their lives. You could walk away from this, and let the police deal with it."

"And what if they never find him? What if I have to spend the rest of my life looking under my bed, in case he's there? I want to come home, Mum. I want to be back with all the rest of you. I never knew what my family meant to me, not until now."

Her mother kissed her and blessed her. "I'll be thinking of you, pet. Every minute of every day."

15

It rained on Saturday afternoon, but by four o'clock the skies began to clear. At four-thirty, a small crowd began to gather at the north end of Roxbourne Park, where a wide area had been taped off for the helicopter to land. A temporary rostrum had been built, with a banner behind it announcing that this was the Creative Hair Stylist of the Year Annual Awards, and two rows of red white and blue bunting. A PA system had been set up, as well as a laser light show, and while everybody waited it boomed out selections from the latest pop charts.

Kelly arrived with DI Brough, in an unmarked police Rover. She was wearing a short, red, sequinned dress and she had sprinkled crimson sparkles in her hair. "The thing is, you have to look as if you're celebrating," Inspector Brough told her. "You have to look as if you're not expecting any trouble at all."

"And what if we *don't* get any trouble?" Kelly asked him.

"Nothing much. You and your friend get a short trip in a helicopter and then we take you back home. I'm afraid the real winner gets the real prize."

"That's a pity," said Susan, as she came up to join them. "I was almost beginning to believe that I *had* won."

DI Brough laid a hand on her shoulder. "If this works – if we can pull this off – you'll get a whole lot more credit than a three-course meal and a tin cup for hairdressing."

"There's nothing demeaning about being a hair stylist," Susan retorted.

"I know. I never said there was. But once in a while we all get a chance to do something extra-special, and this is yours."

"He won't come," Susan whispered to Kelly. "I'll bet you anything he doesn't come."

Kelly looked around at the steadily-gathering crowds of people, and the flags and the spotlights and the criss-crossing lasers. She was carrying Isabel under her arm, and Isabel was alert and alarmed, her ears folded back and her eyes as wide as saucers.

"I don't know why you had to bring that cat," said Susan.

"This cat is the only one who can really sense

him, and knows where he is, and *what* he is."

Susan stopped her. "Do you really believe all of this stuff? I mean, for real?"

"I saw him myself, Susan. I saw him burn up like a torch, and yet he walked away with no burns at all. Kevin, on the other hand—"

"I know," said Susan.

They were still talking when – almost unnoticed – Isabel dropped out of Kelly's arms and hurried off towards the bushes.

"She'll be back," said Kelly. "She's very fastidious about her toilet habits."

A little after four-thirty they heard the *flack-flack-flack* of a helicopter engine, and they saw circles of light hovering in the sky. Everybody stood back a little as a large red-and-white executive helicopter came over the houses backing on to Roxbourne Park, and dipped and circled over the grass.

DI Brough spoke into his intercom. "Charlie Tango landed. Keep the crowds well back. That's right, beyond that perimeter fence. And keep an eye open for anything unusual, any disturbance at all. You hear screaming, you head for that screaming as fast as your regulation shoes will carry you. You see anything dark and hairy, like a gorilla, you go for that, too. And don't make the mistake of under-estimating it. It's bigger than any ape you've ever seen, but it's not as stupid as an ape. It's intelligent and it's ruthless and it's very strong."

"I'm so nervous," Susan told Kelly. "I would be nervous even if we *weren't* trying to find Simon. I mean, if I'd actually won the prize."

Three or four photographers came up to them, wanting to take their pictures. "That's right, darling, put your arms around each other. That's it, lovely! But smile! Come on, smile! You've won a big, big prize! It's not the end of the world!"

A young reporter approached Susan and asked her if she could reveal any advance details of the hairstyle she was planning for James Bond. "Oh," said Susan. "It's like a guided missile. Long and pointy. Bit like your nose, really."

"Make sure you keep those helicopter rotors turning," said DI Brough, into his intercom. "I want it ready to lift off at a second's notice."

Susan and Kelly were ushered towards the helicopter for a final group picture, along with the publisher and editor of *Hair Stylist* and the publicity director for the James Bond movie, and various assorted advertising executives and promoters. Only the publisher and editor of *Hair Stylist* knew that Susan wasn't the real winner of the competition, and what they were here for. They were the only people who didn't smile when their photographs were taken.

"He's not coming," said Susan, as they approached the helicopter. The draught from the rotors made Kelly's reddish-gold hair fly up.

"He *has* to come," Kelly insisted.

"There are too many people here, too many lights. He's not going to risk it."

"He *has* to come," Kelly repeated.

Ned came out of the crowd and ducked under the helicopter's slowly-spinning rotors. "Kelly … your mother told me what you were doing here."

"And what did you think? Girl power strikes again?"

"I think I learned that you're irrepressible; and I'm here to help you, if you'll let me."

"Keep clear of those rotor blades, mate!" shouted the helicopter's co-pilot. "They'll have your head off if you stand up straight!"

"I don't know," said Kelly. "I don't think this is going to work out. There's no sign of Simon, not yet; and we'll have to take off in a minute, or else he'll realize that we've tried to set a trap."

DI Brough came crouching forward. "I'm sorry, Kelly. It looks as if Simon hasn't taken the bait. You'll just have to take off and circle around. They'll drop you off at Northolt Airport and I'll have a car waiting to take you back to your aunt's."

"All right," said Kelly. "I'm sorry that it didn't work out. All these people went to so much trouble, didn't they?" She looked around. "Where's Isabel? I brought my cat here. Has anybody seen her?"

"It's all right," said Ned. "I'll find her for you. Don't you worry. You just go off."

Kelly took hold of Susan's hand and together they started to walk towards the helicopter's open door. The co-pilot jumped out to help them. "This way – that's it – mind the step there."

But just as Kelly was about to climb in, Isabel came tearing across the grass and hid herself behind her legs.

"Isabel – what is it? What's the matter?"

Isabel's tail was standing up like an electrified bush and all her hair was prickling. Kelly picked her up but her muscles were so rigid that she was almost impossible to hold. "Isabel," she soothed her. "What's the matter, Isabel?"

Abruptly, all the floodlights went out. The park was flooded in darkness, and there were cries and shouts from all the people who had come to watch. The only illumination now was the helicopter's flashing navigation lights.

Ned said, "Something's wrong, Kelly! Get into the helicopter! Go on – get into the helicopter now!"

"What? What's wrong?" said Susan, gripping her hand.

"I don't know – there's something here. I don't know what it is, but there's something here."

At that moment, Kelly saw a dark shape approaching through the flashing lights, and she knew what that black shape was. She recognized the hunch of its shoulders and its heavy, hairy body; and as it came nearer she recognized its glaring crimson eyes. It seemed to billow towards her like a thunder-cloud. She heard its voice, too – or its many voices, and they were all roaring at her discordantly. "*Que le diable*..."

Ned tried to intercept it. He dodged to the left, and then to the right, and then he hurled himself straight at it. Kelly shouted out, "*No*!" but she was far too late. The hairy man knocked Ned sideways with a single blow of its arm, and he was flung almost ten metres across the grass. He tried to get up, but then his head flopped back.

"Get in!" the co-pilot urged Kelly. But Kelly said, "Ned – I can't leave Ned!" She turned around and dropped Isabel into Susan's lap, and said, "Look after her. Just, please, look after her."

"Kelly – get in!" Susan begged her. But Kelly closed the cabin door, and said to the co-pilot, "*Go*! But go up slowly. Make as much draught as you can."

"Can't hear you!" said the co-pilot, lifting his headphone away from his ear.

"*Go*!" shrieked Kelly. "*Go! But blow this thing away*!"

She couldn't tell her if he had understood her or not, but he climbed back into the helicopter, and almost immediately its engine burst into a deafening clatter. The rotors whirled faster and faster over Kelly's head and she dropped to her knees in the grass, her hands clamped over her ears.

The hairy man was almost on her. She could see

his shape flickering in the red and white navigation lights. But he was moving more slowly now, because the downdraught from the helicopter's rotor blades was like a Force Ten gale. Kelly felt as if she were going to be blown away across the park. The hairy man trudged forward one step, and then another, but the helicopter hovered right over him, and he could hardly move. Leaves and dust and rubbish were whipped up everywhere, in a whirlwind, and still the helicopter stayed where it was, only three metres above the ground, dipping and yawning and slowly turning in a circle.

Kelly managed to raise her head. The hairy man had almost reached her – but now he, too, had dropped to his knees. Most of the time his face was in darkness, but an occasional flash from the helicopter's tail-lights illuminated his cinder-red eyes and his shark-like mouth. He tore at the turf with his claws, pulling out clumps of mud and grass, and even over the racketing beat of the helicopter's turbine Kelly could hear him whining and gasping for breath.

She tried to get up, but the draught was simply too strong, and it beat her down again. But she heard the hairy man shouting at her, "*I promised, didn't I? I promised that I'd get you, and now I have*!"

As he edged his way nearer, however, a clump of hair flew from the top of his head. More hair was suddenly whipped away from his cheeks, and the bridge of his nose.

"*I will tear you to pieces*!" he shouted at Kelly, but he was suddenly sounding less confident; and instead of coming any nearer, he gripped the ground as if it was all he could do to stay where he was. Above their heads, the helicopter kept circling around, flattening the grass, and keeping both Kelly and Beelzebub flattened down, too.

A flood of hair suddenly blew away from the hairy man's back; and then a whole cloud of it cascaded away from his shoulders. His bright crimson eyes began to dim, and his snake-like tongue was losing its silvery-black lustre.

As more and more hair was blown away from him, Kelly began to recognize the face and features of Simon Crane – pale, intense and full of hate.

He was still patchy with hair, but he was no longer the beast that he was before. All the same, when Kelly tried to crawl away from him, he managed to snatch at her wrist and drag her close. She struggled and kicked, but he lifted his head up and put his mouth close to her ear.

"I should never have taken you on, should I?" he hissed. "You believed in me, that was your trouble. Anybody else would have thought that I was a nightmare, that I was a myth. But I had to pick you, didn't I? That was my mistake. Because when you saw me, you knew that I was real."

Almost all of the devil-hair had been blown away from Simon's body now, but he kept up his grip on Kelly's wrist.

"Let me go, Simon," she told him.

"I didn't want much," he replied. "I wanted a little fame, that's all. A little recognition. I did all the cutting and Richard Walker got the credit. All I wanted was for somebody to say, 'that's a Simon Crane style'. But every time my models appeared in the papers, what did it say? 'Hair by Richard Walker.' Are you surprised that I got jealous? Are you surprised that I wanted what was truly mine?"

"It's over," said Kelly. "You'll have to accept it. It's finished."

"You think so? It will never be finished until Beelzebub sits in his rightful seat among the angels in heaven, and those of us who have served him have their just reward."

"Let go, Simon. They're bringing in the police dogs."

Simon turned his head. Three police dog-handlers were converging on them, and Detective Inspector Brough was following close behind. They reached the perimeter of the helicopter rotors and stopped.

"Give yourself up, Mr Crane!" called DI Brough. "There's nowhere else for you to go!"

"You don't think so?" Simon screamed back at him. "You really don't think so?"

"Come on, Mr Crane. Let the young lady go."

"You're not taking me now, you're not taking me ever! I am the lord of the flies, the demon Beelzebub, the prince of demons!"

"Give it up!" shouted DI Brough. "Give it up and let the girl go!"

With a great effort, Simon climbed to his feet. Then he reached down and seized Kelly under the arms. He pulled her upright, grunting with the strain. The helicopter's rotor blades were flying only a few centimetres above their heads, and Kelly's hair was a whirlwind.

"How about a lift up, my little darling?" said Simon. He gripped her waist and tried to force her upwards, into the spinning blades.

"*No*!" shouted Ned, lunging towards him.

"Your head, lad, watch your head!" called DI Brough.

Ned rugby-tackled Simon at the knees. Simon pitched sideways, dropping Kelly on to the grass. He scrambled forward two or three metres, and then he twisted himself around and stood up, both fists clenched, his face contorted with fury.

Kelly looked up at him, and for a split second she saw his eyes flash crimson – the glaring red of Beelzebub. The demon had possessed him so often now that it didn't need incantations to take over his soul. He was becoming Beelzebub – not from the outside in, but from the inside out.

He opened his mouth wide and roared at them – a roar so loud that it almost drowned out the beating of the helicopter's engine. This wasn't just a choir – this was great groaning organs, and clashing swords, and colliding armour, and all the grinding concerto of war and death and human suffering. This was the real Beelzebub, who had started by indulging one man's greed, and ended up by swamping whole nations with his bloodlust.

"A curse on you, Kelly, and all of yours! A curse on every man and woman who was here tonight! I shall be back to take my revenge, I swear it! And you will never sleep peacefully for the rest of your life!"

It was then that a crosswind caught the helicopter, and it suddenly dipped. One second Simon was standing there screaming at them. The next second there was a sickening *thump* and his head flew off his shoulders and described a high tumbling arc into the trees.

Simon stood there, headless, for almost five seconds, one hand still raised. Blood pumped out of his neck from his still-living heart. Then he collapsed and fell backward, juddering and shuddering as if he had suffered an electric shock. Kelly turned her face away and buried it in Ned's sweater. She had already seen too much horror for one night.

Ned drove her back home to Waverley Road.

"Do you want to come in?" she asked him.

He shook his head. "I don't think so. Maybe some other time."

"This hasn't put you off, has it?"

"Maybe. I don't know. I think I've still got a lot to learn. About girls, you know. How strong they are, and how strong they're not. I think I need to concentrate on my career a little more, before I start to get serious with anybody."

She kissed him on the cheek. "If you change your mind, you know where I live."

"Yes," he said, and kissed her back.

She climbed out of the car, taking Isabel with her. "I just want to thank you for all you've done."

"It was nothing, really. I wish I'd protected you better than I did."

He reached out to stroke Isabel on the head but Isabel hissed at him and wriggled out of Kelly's hands. She ran up the garden path and sat there, waiting to be let in.

"You could have adopted a more sociable animal," Ned told her.

Kelly said nothing, but got out of the car, and closed her door, and gave him a wave goodbye. She watched the red lights of his car disappear around the corner and then she went up the path to join Isabel. Isabel's fur was standing on end and her ears were menacingly flat.

"What is it, kitty? What did you see? Come on, now, you are a silly girl!"

She opened the door and let Isabel into the hallway. Her father was waiting for her in the dining-room, with a big smile and a glass of whiskey in his hand. "How's my girl? It's so good to see you! Why don't you and I sit down now side by side and have a face to face chat?"

The next morning, she woke very late, almost eleven o'clock. Her mother sat on her bed beside her and stroked her hair and kissed her on the forehead. "There's a letter for you," she said.

Kelly sat up in bed. The letter was in a small, lavender-coloured envelope, her name and address written in a neat, sloping script. She couldn't decipher the postmark.

She opened it up and read it, while her mother watched her.

Dearest Kelly,

By the time you read this I shall be very far away. I may even be dead. Soon after you dropped me off I discovered that I had lost my purse in the basement. I decided to walk to your house and ask you to let me back into the salon, so that I could retrieve it. But then I heard noises upstairs. Somebody had climbed into my bedroom window – right up a vertical wall.

I knew that it could only be Simon Crane. He must have returned to the salon and discovered my purse with my address in it. He had changed into a hairy man so that he could take his revenge on me.

I ran. I wanted to warn you but I didn't know your telephone number and I had to get as far away from Rayner's Lane as I possibly could.

Forgive me for letting you down so badly. I only hope that God protects you now and for ever against all of the evil in the world. I have to close now. I can't give you an address because I have to keep on moving. Beelzebub will catch up with me one day, but in the meantime I will continue to fight against his evil till my very last breath. Thank you again for your courage and your strength.

With all my love,
Margaret Paleforth

Kelly looked up at her mother and there were tears

running down her cheeks. "Kelly ... what on earth's the matter?"

Kelly shook her head and folded up the letter and couldn't say anything at all. For the first time in her life, something had happened which she could never explain to parents; something which was hers to deal with, and hers alone.

Ned woke late that morning, too. He felt a prickling sensation on his elbow when he turned over in bed. He rubbed his arm, and at first he put it down to rugby-tackling Simon Crane yesterday evening. But then he pulled up the sleeve of his pyjamas to look at it.

Eight or nine hairs of different colours were growing out of his arm, just above his elbow. He rubbed them again and they felt prickly and coarse, but when he tried to tug one of them out by the roots, he found that he couldn't.

It was that Kelly. She'd infected him. Her and all that hair, down in the basement. She couldn't be trusted, that girl. She and that black fleabag cat of hers. He would have to go round tonight and have a word with her.

He would have to go round tonight and make sure that she got just what she deserved.

Watch out for:

Andrew Matthews

She had lain outside time; now time was against her. The world that she had awoken to was hostile: harsh sunshine, suffocating air, night sky stained orange with artificial light. The conditions did not suit her, and she could find neither comfort nor rest in her surroundings. The food the soldiers had provided was slowly poisoning her. Her digestive system struggled to break down compounds that it was not equipped to deal with, and her strength was at a dangerously low level. If she hibernated she could conserve her energy, but she would not let herself hibernate.

The balance of hormones in her body shifted, sending out an urgent message to the workers who tended the brood chambers. They were to hatch new battalions of soldiers who would grow until they were ready to serve the queen.

This was her final gamble. There were not enough eggs left to mount another search on such a scale and the remaining eggs inside her must be preserved for the foundation of another royal family. Their development depended on special nutrients which she had not yet been able to find, and her need was urgent. Her sole purpose was to pass on the life that she had inherited and without a new queen there could be no new hive, no future generations.

All the individuals in the hive were concentrated on a single goal – that she should die fulfilled.

On Thursday morning there was no escaping Christmas. The bus Jack caught into town had a giant poster of Santa stuck to its side and the driver wore a sprig of holly in his lapel.

Jack gazed out of the window at the sparkling shop decorations that had been up since late October. The streets were crowded with people who were so laden with plastic carriers that Thameswade looked as if it had been invaded by bag ladies. The Octagon was bound to be hell on wheels, and Jack was hardly in the mood for it. There was a lot he needed to sort out: Mum, Dad and Val and the baby, crawlers. Jack didn't know where to start, so he compromised and thought about Beth instead.

He was still thinking about her when her bus pulled in at the station and she got off. They hesitated for a split second, then a hug drew them together.

"I could get to like this," Beth said into Jack's neck.

"So could I," Jack said into her hair, "once I've worked out what we are. I mean, are we friends or an item?"

Beth looked up and flashed him a wicked grin. "We're sort of a cross between the two. We're a fritem."

Jack laughed and lowered his head, meaning to give her a kiss.

Beth pressed her hand over his mouth. "Let's not rush things, Jack!"

"Why not?" said Jack. Beth's fingers turned it into, "Mph?"

"Our first kiss is going to be special and it's definitely not going to happen in Thameswade bus station!"

Beth took her hand away.

Jack blushed; he felt as if he'd spoiled things by being greedy. "Sorry!"

"Don't be! Kissing is good. Right idea, wrong location."

"What's the right location – in a field of ripe wheat, under a full moon?"

"More like on top of Beacon Hill in the middle of a thunderstorm. Save romance till later, right now I'm hot to shop!"

On the way to the Octagon, Jack gave Beth the details of Dr Richardson's e-mail about the crawler.

Beth said, "Wow!" and, "Ugh!" in the right places, and then Jack suddenly stopped in mid-sentence.

"Something bothering you, Jack?"

"We're holding hands!"

"Mm, so we are."

"When did that happen?"

"Don't ask me, I've only just noticed myself. Feels all right, doesn't it?"

"You're not worried?"

"Should I be?"

"If anybody from your school sees us, they'll think we're a couple."

"Well, we *are* a couple! A couple of crazy mixed-up kids lost in a world that doesn't understand. Would you prefer the secret approach – like Romeo and Juliet?"

"No! I know it's one of the world's great love stories, but somehow the thought of being dead in a tomb doesn't do it for me."

The Octagon didn't do it for Jack either. The noise level inside was brutal, a brain-numbing mixture of garbled voices and muzak. Beth grabbed a guide to the mall and they retreated to a coffee bar inside a book shop to consult it. The coffee bar was relatively peaceful: no one shouted and the background music was provided by a CD selection of string quartets.

Jack licked cappuccino froth off his top lip and said, "What's the plan?"

"It isn't a plan, it's a campaign," said Beth. "My dad's present is sorted, so it's off to the Body Shop to get smellies for my mum, the Disney Store for my kid brother and Common Scents for Tom. He could use a change of aftershave."

"And Tom is?"

"Mum's new feller. He's coming round for Christmas dinner."

Jack knew that Beth's parents were divorced, but he hadn't liked to ask her too many questions about it. They'd compared notes on their parents, but Beth hadn't gone into any painful details. Now Jack felt he could probe a little deeper.

"How are you with Tom?"

"He's OK, a bit boring but Mum seems keen. Almost as keen as he is."

"D'you think they'll get married?"

"I wish they would – Tom's loaded. No worries about tuition fees when I'm a student if those two get hitched. How about your Dad and Val?"

"They haven't mentioned anything. Val's first marriage failed, like Dad's. I think they're – once bitten twice shy, you know?"

Beth finished her coffee and consulted her watch. "Right, time to get started. Once the family's presents are out of the way, I can get down to the real stuff!"

"What's the real stuff?"

"*My* presents. I can't trust my mum and my

brother to get me the things I want, so I buy them and they wrap them up."

"Doesn't that take away the surprise on Christmas Day?"

"Yeah," Beth agreed, "but it also guarantees that I'm not disappointed."

Two hours later Jack was on the sixth floor of the Octagon, dazed by lights and people and nursing an ache in the backs of both knees. He'd passed on going into HMV, saying that he needed a break, and was leaning against a brushed aluminium safety rail, taking in the crowds swirling around below him. From that height the shoppers looked like ants.

Beth staggered out of HMV and slumped against Jack, resting her head on his left shoulder. "That's it, believe it or not!" she panted. "I've crossed the last item off my list and I'm starving."

"Where would you like to eat? There are twelve restaurants in here, plus three burger bars, two pizza huts, a fried chicken shack, a—"

"Isn't there a greasy spoon we could go to in town? Now I'm all shopped-out, I've had it with this place."

"There's a sandwich bar near the railway station. It's a bit basic, but they do a mean bacon roll."

"Anywhere, as long as it's not—"

Beth was interrupted by a clatter and a chorus of shrill screams.

Jack glanced down. People were scattering like spilled peas.

"What the—?" Jack muttered, and then he spotted the reason for the disturbance.

The cover had fallen off an air-conditioning vent above a jeweller's shop on the third floor, and crawlers were cascading out of it. Some were dropping on to the floor, others running up the walls towards the roof.

Beth's jaw dropped. "Jack, is that … are they…?"

"Crawlers," Jack said grimly. "We're out of here!"

"I can't move!" Beth wailed. "My legs won't work!"

A grey shape fell past her face and landed near her feet. Beth automatically stamped on it. Jointed legs writhed either side of the sole of her Doc Martens.

"Your legs are working now," said Jack. "Come on!"

He seized Beth's arm and tugged.

"Where are you taking me, Jack? The escalators are that way."

"Everybody's going to try and use the escalators, and they'll form a bottleneck. There's a lift down there to the right. If we luck in, it'll be empty."

"And if we luck out?"

"According to Dr Richardson, we'll be eaten."

They ran.

Crawlers were everywhere, darting across the patterned marble of the floor, sliding down from the roof on threads, jumping on to the people who were fleeing from them.

Jack and Beth reached the lift. Jack hit the down button and it lit up. A bell pinged, the doors opened. He bundled Beth inside and stepped in behind her. The doors closed and the lift began to descend.

"That was close!" Jack said. "Another couple of minutes and—"

Beth's eyes were fixed to the roof of the lift, her pupils shrunk in terror. "Jack?" she said quietly. "We've got company."

Jack heard the clicking of the crawler before he saw it. It was in the centre of the roof, testing the air with its antennae to try and fix its exact position; the downward motion of the lift had temporarily disorientated it.

"There's a fire extinguisher by your right foot, Beth. Can you reach it?"

"What if the crawler goes for me?"

"We'll give it two targets, get it really confused. When you go right, I'll go left – OK? One, two, *three*!"

The crawler's legs bristled as it homed in on Jack, keeping its mandibles pointed at him.

"It's ignoring me, Jack!" Beth said. "It's after you." She ripped the extinguisher from its mount and held it in both hands. "How do these things work?"

"I don't know. Read the instructions!"

Beth didn't have time to read anything. The lift

was slowing down; the crawler gathered itself to spring.

Beth flipped the extinguisher over so its base was uppermost and slammed it against the roof.

The crawler burst, body fluids spraying out in a ragged stain around its shattered body.

The lift stopped and the doors parted. Beth bent over to retrieve her shopping.

"What are you doing?" Jack gasped.

"I'm not leaving these presents behind. No dumb insect is going to spoil my Christmas!"

They walked out of the lift into one of the Octagon's main entrance lobbies. It was packed with shoppers who were bunched around the exits, trying to fight their way outside, their eyes round and blank with panic.

Jack saw an emergency exit sign and yanked Beth over to it. They went down a short, sloping passageway, through a fire door and into total chaos.

The roads around the Octagon were gridlocked. Car horns beeped, headlights flashed; two police cars and an ambulance added their wailing sirens to the din. People who didn't know what was happening stopped to stare; those who did know ran and kept on running.

"Where now?" Beth shouted.

"Thamesmead Park. We'll follow the river to the industrial estate. I'll ring Val on my mobile and she'll pick us up from there."

"Are you sure that way's safe?"

"No, but if you've got a better suggestion, now's the time to make it."

Beth squeezed his hand. "I'm with you, Jack."

Jack gave Beth a smile that he hoped was reassuring.

Point Horror Unleashed

CALLING ALL POINT HORROR FANS

[illegible]

At Gehenna's Door

[illegible]

Transformer

[illegible]

The Carver

[illegible]

House of Bones

[illegible]

Darker

[illegible]

The Ghost Wife

[illegible]

Blood Sinister

The Vanished

[illegible]

The Hanging Tree

Fright Train

[illegible]

Catchman

[illegible]

Point Horror Unleashed.

It's one step beyond.